The Man
Who Saved
SPAIN

A Latter-Day Baron Munchausen

Hugh Hosch

authorHOUSE®

AuthorHouse™
1663 Liberty Drive
Bloomington, IN 47403
www.authorhouse.com
Phone: 1 (800) 839-8640

Published by AuthorHouse   06/29/2017

ISBN: 978-1-5246-9383-1 (sc)
ISBN: 978-1-5246-9382-4 (e)

Library of Congress Control Number: 2017908413

Print information available on the last page.

Any people depicted in stock imagery provided by Thinkstock are models, and such images are being used for illustrative purposes only. Certain stock imagery © Thinkstock.

This book is printed on acid-free paper.

For Nat Peters, my inspiration for "the new Cid"

In Spain, the dead are more alive than the dead of any other country in the world.
-- Federico Garcia Lorca

AUTHOR'S NOTE

The main character of this book, a professor of Medieval Spanish Literature, speaks fluent Spanish, but of a Medieval Spanish variety. Since the book is in English, I have tried to capture the feeling of his speech by using a form of Medieval English for the professor's spoken words.

Lionel Sidney Camp as a student in Spain in 1960

"El Cid Campeador II" on his return to Spain

Sidney's destinations in Spain

FOREWORD

Professor Sidney Camp understood the Spanish language. Indeed, he was the most revered professor of Medieval Spanish Literature at Northwestern Central Kansas Southern State University. True, he spoke Spanish the way Shakespeare spoke English, in antiquated fashion (to us today), but Spaniards could usually understand him. So when the tough-looking, thirtyish and mustachioed man of the Spanish National Intelligence Center (CNI) in Madrid who leaned over the back of the straight-backed chair in the windowless room shouted at him, Sidney understood the man.

"*Señor*, we believe you are an enemy of Holy Spain!" A gold crucifix dangled on a chain from the man's neck.

"Nay, nay, I loveth Spain!" cried Sidney in his medieval Spanish, truly perplexed.

"Then why were you trying to damage our wind turbines?" shouted the CNI man. Sweat formed on his upper lip.

"Twast a mistaketh!" wailed Sidney. "A no more brain than stone mistaketh!"

"Why do you talk so funny?"

And so began Sidney Camp's return to Spain – for the first time since 1960.

CHAPTER 1

Professor Lionel Sidney Camp, a confirmed bachelor, had been at Northwestern Central Kansas Southern University, home of the Fighting Wombats, in one capacity or another since 1959. Majoring as an undergraduate in Spanish literature, he took his first and – up to now, only – trip to Spain at the end of his freshman year, in 1960. He traveled over much of the country and loved every minute of it. Upon his return to NWCKSC (It was *college* then, not yet university), he continued his education in "Spanish lit", moved on to graduate school, and in time went on to become, first, an instructor, and subsequently, a professor. Now he was the doyen of all the school's language professors, the region's leading expert in Medieval Spanish Literature. And for the first time since 1960, he was going back to Spain!

Sidney was a relatively mild-mannered fellow, but his physique was misleading: he was big, six-four, two-fifty, and he had an amazing wild crop of curly gray hair atop his head. And a very commanding voice: deep, resonant and loud. Students in the back row could hear him clearly.

Although his first name was Lionel, the professor did not like it nor use it. It was his father's name, and he wanted his own. The name Lionel also reminded him of an electric train set he had when he was a child. So he went by Sidney, or Sid.

And now he was going back to Spain! Sidney was excited, although he did not know what to expect. He had not kept up with the goings-on in Spain since his trip in 1960. Rather, he had concentrated on his pet subject – Medieval Spainish Literature, that glorious period comprising roughly the thirteenth through the fifteenth centuries, the greatest work of the epoch being the epic poem *Cantar de Mio Cid,* written in about 1140 by an unknown poet. Sidney gloried –nay, wallowed – in this stuff. But he was blissfully ignorant of most of what had gone on in Spain – or in Europe or anywhere else, for that matter – in the interim. On his return to Spain, Sidney would truly be a babe in the woods.

CHAPTER 2

Sidney's first trip had been "by boat" (ship, actually), several days' tourist class passage on a vessel of American Export Lines which docked in Gibraltar. From there Sidney had traveled by bus to Seville, and thence by train to Madrid. It had taken forever, so he was quite naturally stunned when now it all took place quickly and comfortably, with travel from New York to Madrid via a sleek new jet airplane in just a few hours. Sidney remembered the old, slow, coal-burning locomotive from Seville to Madrid and the soot blowing through the passenger cars' open windows. What a difference!

Anyway, here Sidney was in Madrid. He went to a small *pensión* he remembered from 1960, a hole-in-the-wall place called el Pensión Jamal Sabla, just off the

Puerta del Sol in the city center and run by a family of Spanish Moroccans. He remembered paying fifteen pesetas, or twenty-five cents U.S., for his bathless room in 1960; now it was fifty euros, or about fifty-three dollars U.S. What was going on? And what was all this euro stuff about? What had happened to pesetas?

Well, he would have to get about. And now that he was at least relatively affluent – certainly compared to his student days in 1960 – he figured he could afford to rent a car in which to roam the land. So he walked to a U-Drive office near the Plaza de España and, feeling rather carefree, rented a white, canvas-topped Jeep, automatic transmission, four wheel drive, the works. Then he began making his plans to travel about Spain.

Sidney spent a couple of days just re-exploring Madrid, and then on the third day he drove across the Manzanares River, passing through the little town of Consuegra, in La Mancha. Eventually, off to the right along the top of a ridge, he saw a line of modern wind turbines, those white, three-bladed propeller wind machines atop tall poles, generators of electric power. He had read in a magazine on the airplane coming over that Spain was the world's fifth biggest producer of wind power, and that a proposal was in the works to build the greatest wind power production facility in the world, in the sea off southwestern Spain, on the spot of the 1805 Battle of Trafalgar. The proposal

DRAWN FROM MEMORY
BY L. SID CAMP —
AFTER MY ADVENTURE

Bibieca, Sidney's rented jeep

had been met with strong opposition from Cadiz and towns in that region, and even by the British, who feared that any such development might destroy archeological evidence of the historic battle. But "progress" is hard to stop, and Sidney, being nothing if not a rigid traditionalist in all things Spanish, worried. He stopped his Jeep off the highway and stared at the line of wind turbines cresting the distant hill.

"God alast!" he cursed in his Medieval Spanish, unlike him. He let out the clutch and had the Jeep charge off the road's shoulder, headed for the ridge. He shifted into four- wheel-drive for better traction, as he started up the hill. He wanted to "see what made these things tick." Near the top, his vehicle plunged into a gully and Sidney banged his forehead – hard – against the windshield. The Jeep stalled, and Sidney lay back against his headrest, stunned. He sat there for some time, trying to gather his faculties.

Eventually he "came to" and stared maliciously at the big, white wind turbines. Enemies of traditional Spain! He turned the ignition key and re-cranked the Jeep's engine. Then, shifting down into the automatic transmission's first gear, he "gunned it" and worked his way out of the gully, heading toward the nearest white pole. As he neared the base of the wind turbine, Sidney was surprised to see just how thick it was.

DRAWN FROM MEMORY
BY L. SID CAMP —
AFTER MY ADVENTURE

Wind turbines

No telephone pole, this; it was a good five feet across. Nevertheless, his brain still clouded with madness from his crash, he rammed the front bumper of the Jeep against the base of the wind turbine. It seemed to do no damage, so he backed up and charged the wind machine again. And again. And again. Until he finally slumped over in his seat, exhausted – and dizzy. He passed out at the wheel.

When Sidney came to, he was looking into the chest of a man with a badge which read *Guardia del Parque, Emilio Perez.* The man wearing it spoke, in Spanish.

"*Señor,* I must call the police. You have tried to destroy government property."

"Oh, the horror!" groaned Professor Sidney Camp, rubbing his forehead.

CHAPTER 3

Professor Lionel Sidney Camp decided it might be a good idea for him to "get out of Dodge", as his students might put it. Dodge City was, of course, in Kansas – although this was Spain. Oh, well.

Sidney drove his Jeep to the front of el Pensión Jamal Sabla and loaded his one bag into the back. He had not been humored when the CNI man had laughed and said that *Jamal Sabla* in Arabic meant *Camel Dung*. But at least the creature had finally let him go – after making a notation in a black book. He would have to be careful henceforth.

As he waited for his bill to be prepared, Sidney read a local Spanish newspaper. There, just below an article on just how much Spanish businessmen resented "interference from Brussels", a piece said Spain's economy was really in the tank. In fact, it was so bad the European Union was talking about throwing Spain out of the EU,

DRAWN FROM MEMORY
BY L. SID CAMP —
AFTER MY ADVENTURE

Pancho Zinsano

along with Greece – and maybe others. Spanish governments were coming and going like the Italians used to do.

When he went back out to his Jeep, Sidney found a paunchy, youngish-middleaged man wearing a silly hat and leaning on a fender. The man spoke, in rather poor Spanish.

"Oh, *señor*! Are you by chance traveling to another city?"

Sidney hesitated. "Uh, well, aye, I am," he replied.

"And where might that be?" inquired the stranger.

"Well, uh, I am not sure. Mayhap, er, Barcelona?" That had been the second place he had visited in 1960, after Madrid.

"Ah. Barcelona! That is most fine! May I please to beg a ride with you, *señor*? My name is Pancho Zinsano and I know all the highways and byways of Spain. I am a true *pícaro!* I can help you immensely!"

Sidney pondered this information, then decided, hell, why not? I can always chuck the guy out later if I want to.

"Very well. Receivith it. Alloweth us wend." Pancho

figured that meant okay, so he climbed into the Jeep's passenger seat. He had but a small wad of belongings wrapped in a large, paisley-patterned handkerchief and tied onto the end of a long stick.

"We art off!" cried Sidney, and they departed.

CHAPTER 4

Sidney and Pancho were preparing to drink some bottled water at one of those stand-up tables at a state-of-the-art rest stop just off the toll road *autopista*, a modern superhighway which amazed the professor. He remembered nothing but two-lane roads abounding in potholes. Road repair crews had relied on burros hauling big baskets of molten tar, one basket per beast's side, which matter was shoveled out and into the gaps in the highway by weary workers wearing towels on their heads and necks, to ward off the brilliant sun. Now, up-to-date, yellow, motorized road equipment did a much better job in a fraction of the time. Outside the rest stop, the landscape looked like desert land in Arizona or New Mexico.

Pancho interrupted his reverie. "What is your name, *señor?*" he asked politely. "You know mine. I am Pancho Zinsano, *pícaro extraordinario.* With whom do I have the honor of traveling the *carreteras* of our wonderful España?"

Sid paused, then replied, "I am L. Sidney Camp, a professeth'r of Medieval Spanish did light'rature at a university in the United States. Most people calleth me Sidney, or just Sid. This is mine own first trippeth to Spain since 1960."

Pancho's eyes grew wide. "El Cid Camp!" he whispered. "El Cid Campeador! The warrior lord who made Spain great so long ago! You have returned! Reincarnated! You have come back as a *yanqui* to save our poor nation in its hour of need! Oh, of course! Just look at you! Big, tall, with a powerful speaking voice – a voice, which I may say, *señor,* sounds like that of El Cid of the eleventh century! The antiquated words, the ancient diction, like a prophet of old! Oh, *señor!* Are you truly El Cid Campeador, come to rescue us at this time of national peril, as you did my home town of Valencia so long ago? Can it be true?"

Sidney was more than a little embarrassed by his new friend's ebullience and wonder. He of course knew all about the historical figure Rodrigo Diaz de Vivar,

Spain's greatest hero of the eleventh century, best known from the medieval epic poem, *El Cantar de Mio Cid*. If non-scholars in America remembered him at all, it was probably from that 1961 Charleton Heston Hollywood movie, *El Cid*, when, in the final act, a mortally wounded Cid is strapped onto his war horse and successfully "leads" his troops into battle at the siege of Valencia, the enemy routed by an army led by a man apparently risen from the dead.

"Oh, doth not beest fartuous," sighed the professor, reaching for his bottle of water. Pancho was already drinking his own. Then Sidney looked at the bottle he had plucked from the rest stop's beverage shelf. He had grabbed a similar sized bottle of white wine in error.

"Oh, lief," he said, examining the wine bottle. "'T seemeth I hast wine, not wat'r."

Pancho's eyes grew even wider, if that were possible, and he fell to his knees at Sidney's feet. "*Mi señor!*" he gasped. "You have turned water into wine! Before my eyes! You are truly el Cid Campeador! Come to save *España!*"

DRAWN FROM MEMORY
BY L. SID CAMP —
AFTER MY ADVENTURE

Charleton Heston as el Cid Campeador

Sidney was really embarrassed now. Other people in the little store-restaurant were staring at the middle-aged man on his knees before the big foreigner. "Receiveth up, Pancho!" he shouted, his basso voice booming and his hands motioning "Get up!" "F'r God's sake!" Reluctantly, Pancho resumed a standing position, hunched over, hat in hand; Sidney could tell he was shaken. The onlookers in the store, some six or eight of them, watched, interested.

Now, one of those onlookers just happened to be a woman reporter for a Zaragoza newspaper – and she instinctively knew this would make terrific copy, especially in these trying times. The return of el Cid! The great warrior who had defeated the Aragonese enemy while in the employ of the Taifa of Zaragoza in the year 1081, before going on to even greater exploits elsewhere in Spain! Ha! The reporter had her notebook out, writing furiously.

Sidney went to the bathroom, then emerged to see Pancho speaking wildly to the reporter, who was smiling and scribbling like mad in her notebook. When the reporter saw Sidney returning, she snapped a picture of him with her phone camera. A furious Sidney dragged Pancho out of the rest stop building and held open the door to the Jeep's passenger side for him. Before closing the door, a now calming down Sid saw some humor in the whole thing.

"You know," he said to himself in English. "El Cid's horse was named Babieca. Yes. Yes, I shall name my trusty vehicle Babieca!" And with a laugh, he piled into the driver's seat, cranked the Jeep's engine and headed east to Barcelona with Pancho.

CHAPTER 5

"What doth thee cullionly, th're art nay bullfights in Cataluña?" Sidney challenged the hotel concierge. In Barcelona, he had decided to up his grade of hostelry; no more Pensión Camel Dung for him. Pancho was pleased when he heard Sidney ask at Reception for "a servant's room" for him, as well. He had digs! The Colón, opposite the great cathedral in the city's *Barrio Gótico*, was nice. But this next bit of news wasn't, at least not to Sidney.

"But it is true, *señor*!" said the female *concerje*. "The last bullfight here was in 2011! The Generalitat, the Catalán government; it has banned them!" The young woman twitched nervously.

"But wherefore?" cried Sidney. "The corrida – the bullfight – has been an integral parteth of Spanish culture since the year 1133, at the timeth of King Alfonso VIII!

Wherefore, at which hour I wast here in 1960, I wenteth to the corrida ev'ry Sunday at the Plaza Monumental! And oft to a *nocturno* at Plaza Arenas on Sunday night! Barcelona hadst m're bullfights than Madrid!"

The concierge, in an effort to calm down her guest, sighed and leaned across her counter, conspiratorally. "*Señor*! I understand your concern! Look, I myself am from Córdoba, in Andalucía, where everybody loves the *corrida*! When I visit my relatives there, we all go to *la plaza de toros* as a family! My grandmother, my children, everybody! But not here, no, *señor*."

"But wherefore?" Sidney almost screamed out. "Tis an essential parteth of the culture of Spain!"

"*Señor, señor*," said the hotel lady, flapping her hands downward, as though to quieten him. "*Si*, you are correct. But the Catalunya of today in not the Cataluña of 1960! As a true Spaniard, and not as a Catalán, I will tell you that I think the Catalán government banned the corrida precisely *because* it is part of the culture of Spain!

Hotel Colón, Barcelona

"If *water* were thought to be a thing of Spanish culture, I firmly believe they would try to ban water, too! What they really want is full independence from Spain, with no trace of Spain remaining!" The woman leaned back and puffed out her cheeks, then added, "Just look about you, *señor.* In the streets, you will see no street signs in Castellano, or Spanish. Just Catalán. You will see some in French, even English. But no Spanish. By law, half the films shown in local cinemas must be in Catalán. We even had a popular strike of the people against the cinemas; they want to see movies they can understand. Not Catalán. After all, in Barcelona, 98% of the people speak Spanish, with only 50% speaking Catalán. All government business is done exclusively in Catalán. It is a thing of misplaced pride, *señor.*"

Pancho interrupted. "It is true all over Spain, *señor*! I have told you I am from Valencia, and even there the government uses Valenciano, not Castellano, for all things official. It is similar to Catalán but somewhat different. I and my family do not use it. *Claro*, I don't even know it – as most of the people who live there do not."

Sidney thought for a moment, then muttered, "This the horror hast did get to cease!"

CHAPTER 6

Sidney and Pancho were sitting at a table in a Starbuck's near their hotel. Sidney was looking at a local newspaper which was printed in Catalán. He had not bought it – it had simply been left there on the table by an earlier patron.

"Behold at this garbage!" snarled the professor. "Who ist reads this alas? And what valorous is this no more brain than stone gibb'rish to anybody, once those gents leaveth Barcelona? Nobody – and a cullionly nobody – reads 'r speaks this tush tush anywh're else! And t'wast nev'r here before!"

Pancho smiled apologetically and shrugged his shoulders. "Well, *Señor* el Cid, as they say, 'When in Rome'..."

"But we art *not* in Rome!" Sidney shouted, spilling his Mongolian dandelion chocolate frappé and causing a few heads to turn. "And besides, in Rome those gents speaketh Italian. And Italian is a language – a *real* language! Doth thee realizeth yond Alfonso X, the fath'r of Spanish prose, is belike rolling ov'r in his grave?"

"*Si, señor!*" said Pancho, then changing that to "Uh, no, *señor*! That is, I do not know, *señor!*"

"Well, I doth!" retorted Sidney, gritting his teeth and looking back and disdainfully flipping a page of the Catalán newspaper. On the inside, a full page displayed the pictures and names of the members of the Generalitat, or local government. They all seemed to have Spanish surnames and odd-looking first names, like Gruxcect Garcia.

"Here art the culprits!" he cried, jabbing a forefinger at the page. "A sorry-looking bunch if't be true ever I did see one!"

"*Sí, señor,*" replied Pancho.

"Behold here!" said Sidney, pointing to the photo of one of the members of the Generalitat. "As most wondrous I can deciper this gibb'rish, 't sayeth this shaved-head thug is the Minister of Foreign Affairs! How can a city has't its owneth Minister of Foreign Affairs? Ridiculous!"

"*Si, señor,*" said Pancho.

Sidney turned another page and, to his horror, saw his own image staring out at him. The photo had obviously been taken in that rest stop near Zaragoza. Since he couldn't read the Catalán, he jumped up and went to the Starbucks' counter, where he bought a Spanish newspaper (the employees all spoke Castellano) and began rapidly riffling through it. He looked past the usual article about the EU in Brussels making life difficult for Spaniards. Then, sure enough, there was the same slightly-out-of-focus photograph of him taken at the rest stop. This time he could read the story:

RETURN OF EL CID?
Norteamericano Claims to Be
Reincarnation of 11th c. Hero

At an autopista rest stop near Zaragoza, our reporter by chance encountered a big, elderly norteamericano who claims to be the reincarnated legendary, eleventh century warrior of song and story, Rodrigo Diaz de Vivar, better known as el Cid Campeador. Even his vehicle, an open-topped, white Jeep, is said to be named Bibieca, which was also the name of the original Cid's horse. His manservant, a middleaged valenciano called Pancho Zinsano, swears that the man's name really is el Cid Campeador, and his master apparently speaks fluent medieval castellano.

What is this medieval hero doing in Spain today? His companion says his employer is on a holy quest to restore Spain's former glory, banishing languages other than castellano and restoring "the old, traditional ways." His compañero Pancho also swears that he witnessed "el Cid" turn water into wine, there in the rest stop.

The article went on to describe Sidney and Pancho, and to mention that they were headed to Barcelona.

"This is utterly ridiculous!" asserted the professor. Pancho said nothing.

Sidney then sat there, unspeaking, for a moment. Then he leaned back in his chair and said, "Well, haply I can useth this. But in any case, I knoweth what I am going to doth. Pancho! Doth thee knoweth where is the headquarters of this Generalitat, 'r whatev'r the no more brain than stone place is hath called?"

"Uh, no, *señor.*"

Sidney stood up quickly, knocking his chair backward

and onto the floor. "Well, we shall findeth it!" People stared at him.

"We shall?" asked Pancho, his eyes wide.

"Aye! We art going to yond toy government building and we art going to crisp house! Spain might not but not has't to tolerate these ...these...traitors!" Sidney stormed out of the Starbucks with Pancho in tow, a man on a mission. He had torn the article about el Cid out of the newspaper and stuffed it into a coat pocket.

CHAPTER 7

Sidney and Pancho were in front of their hotel in the old *Barrio Gótico.* The Colón faced onto the huge Pla (or Plaza) de la Seu, with the massive Gothic cathedral opposite. Professor L. Sidney Camp pulled a folded-up city map from his jacket pocket and began to scour it. "Hark!" he exclaimed. "There t'is! Practically 'round the corner! Alloweth us wend!"

They headed up the busy sidewalk, but something caught Sidney's eye: a large letter A with a circle around it, spray-painted on walls here and there. But then he stopped at a souvenir shop purveying junk to tourists. There were small Catalán and Spanish flags, miniature stuffed fighting bulls (but no bullfights!), tiny Toledo swords, cheap reproductions of ancient flintlock pistols – and, on the sidewalk out front of the shop, a felt board covered with fake "gold" lapel pins of all sorts. There were cameos of the king and queen, bas-relief miniatures of castanets, leather wine bottles, or *botas*, guitars, and so on. But what caught Sidney's eye was a pin shaped like a double yoke for oxen and a sprawl of bunched arrows in the center.

"Behold, Pancho!" cried Sidney. "The yoke and arrows symbol of King Fernando and Queen Isabel! From the fifteenth century!" He plucked the gold-looking pin from the board and held it up to his jacket lapel. "I wilt has't this!" He rushed into the shop with the pin – and bought it. He came out wearing the pin and a big grin.

"Doth thee liketh it? He asked Pancho. "'T hast most wondrous significance," he added. "The yokes represent the produceth of the landeth, while the arrows representeth the might of the state."

"Er, *sí, señor,* but . . ." Pancho stammered.

"But?" said Sidney. "But what?" He looked down at his new pin.

"Er, *señor,*" mumbled the putative manservant of El Cid Campeador, "I think perhaps you should know something."

Sidney looked up, at Pancho. "Doth I knoweth what, Pancho?" he asked, only half attuned to his friend's concern.

"Er, *señor*, during the Franco years that yoke and arrows thing was the official symbol of the Falangista Party. Some people say it is the symbol of *España fasçista.* I'm not sure it would be a good idea to wear it around everywhere. Especially here in Barcelona, where General Franco was, er, not too popular."

"Poppycock!" retorted the professor of Medieval Spainish Literature, in English. "Tis the well-known symbol of *Los Reyes Católicos* Fernando and Isabel! Everyone knoweth yond!" And with that, they headed off, quick time, for the building housing the Generalitat of Catalunya, Sidney proudly wearing the pin on his jacket lapel.

DRAWN FROM MEMORY
BY L. SID CAMP —
AFTER MY ADVENTURE

Sidney's lapel pin

CHAPTER 8

The two men walked at a brisk pace, Pancho hurrying to keep up with the long-legged professor. Soon they entered the Pla de Saint Jaume, or la Plaza de San Jaime, as Sidney would have preferred. There across the square was a very attractive four-story building in the Renaissance style, cream colored and with a dome atop it. The Catalán flag – alternating red and yellow horizontal stripes – flew from the top of the building. Two soldiers with slung carbines flanked the ornate doorway.

"This is't, Pancho," Sidney said, a gleam in his eye.

"*Si, señor!*"

"Alloweth us wend!" Sidney strode determinedly across the square, Pancho trying to keep up.

At the main entrance were a few steps, and Sidney bounded up them.

DRAWN FROM MEMORY
BY L. SID CAMP —
AFTER MY ADVENTURE

The Generalitat, Barcelona

"*Señor!*" called out one of the guards, but Sidney continued on inside. Pancho hesitatingly did the same, although the soldiers were not really paying him attention.

When he got to a reception desk inside, Sidney pulled the newspaper article about him being el Cid from a jacket pocket and held it out for the man behind the desk to see. The man looked rather dumbfounded.

"I am L. Sidney Camp!" asserted Sidney in medieval Castellano. "I am here to seeth the president of this would-be state! Anon!"

The receptionist, a small, bald-headed man about sixty, looked goggle-eyed at the newspaper article and photograph held in front of his face, then at Sidney, and then to a staircase to his left. One of the soldiers from the front door was running up to the desk.

"Aha!" cried Sidney, already taking the steps to the left two at a time. The soldier pursued him, demanding he stop – to no avail. On the second floor (first floor, in European parlance) Sidney saw a grand doorway halfway down the hall. As with the front entrance, two soldiers flanked it, standing at parade rest, beside two Catalán flags. Before they knew what had happened, the professor had whisked by them and was in the anteroom of the president's chamber. The three soldiers – two from the

president's door and the one from the front entrance –
rushed after him, their weapons now unslung.

Here another receptionist sat behind a desk, this time
a woman. She stood up, alarmed at this intrusion. Sidney's
deep voice boomed out.

"I hest to seeth the president! I am L. Sidney Camp!"

At that moment, the president just happened to open
the door to exit his inner sanctum, and what with all
the hubbub about him, what he heard was, "I am el Cid
Campeador!" The president also saw the newspaper
article with photograph which was being held out front
by Sidney like a road sign, and the heavy black words in
the headline, "El Cid." The president, a youngish-looking
man with lots of black hair parted down the middle and
with Hitler-style bangs covering his forehead on both the
right and left sides, had his mouth open. The three soldiers
ran up and were in the process of grabbing at Sidney, but,
surprisingly, the president held up a hand and in some
strange language bade them stop, which they did, although
nervously. The president spoke in the gobbledegook
language and when Sidney asked in Spanish what he was
saying, the head Catalán switched to perfect Castellano,
asking what it was he wanted, although he did goggle
upon spotting Sidney's lapel pin.

"I am here to putteth Spain – and yond enwheels Cataluña – backeth on the proper path!" he declared. I refer to the path of el Cid and to yond of the Spain which at one timeth did rule the world!"

The female receptionist said something in Catalán to the president but, smiling, he patted her on the shoulder and shook his head.

"I will give you two minutes," he said to Sidney, and then waved him into his office. "I have heard of you," he was heard to say, before his double doors clicked shut, closing out the soldiers and everyone else. Somewhere along the way, Pancho seemed to have gotten lost in the shuffle.

The two men remained standing, the president with his arms crossed and look of humor and bewilderment on his face.

"So, *Señor* el Cid? What have you to say?" He glared nervously at Sidney's new lapel pin.

"*Señor presidente*," said Sidney, "I am here to beseech thee to give up this folly of persuing a path of independence for Cataluña. Bethink of the Spain of its glory days, at which hour Spain did rule the world! Not with't broken into tiny bits, weilding nay power 'r influenceth. And thy tiny bit with a language – 'r a dialect – yond nobody else on earth speaks! Spain can beest most wondrous again! But not as a fragmented hodgepodge. Bethink of *El Cantar de Mio Cid*! Bethink of Cervantes! Of *Los Reyes Católicos*! Of Cortez, Pizarro, Balboa! Of . . ."

"Your two minutes are up," declared *el presidente*, smirking and glancing at his wristwatch, a gold Rolex. Then he shouted something in Catalán and the doors immediately crashed opened, admitting the two soldiers.

"But, sir," began Sidney, but the guards had him out of the room before he could say "Juanito Robinson," or whatever it was they would say in Catalán. They frogmarched him along the hall, down the staircase, and along the entrance hall to the front door, where Pancho was waiting on the sidewalk outside, talking to a gaggle of reporters with microphones and notebooks at the ready. Some TV vans were pulled up in front of the building and cameramen were zooming their lenses in on Pancho. How on earth do these people appear so quickly, just out of the blue, Sidney wondered.

"*Señor* Cid! *Señor* Cid!" The reporters all shouted at once, thrusting microphones in Sidney's face. "What did you and the president discuss?" "Are you really el Cid?" "What is your goal?" And other shouted questions.

Sidney saw his chance. "We did discuss the ending

of the searcheth for independence on Cataluña's parteth, and the effort to once again maketh a united, grandiose Spain!" The reporters went wild, scribbling, filming and shouting more questions. But Sidney and Pancho now strolled down the sidewalk, the mob of reporters continuing to call out queries, the photographers – still and video – still snapping and whirring away. Finally, when the questions began to grow repetitious, Sidney flagged down a taxi and he and Pancho roared off.

And that night his story was on the local TV news – three channels, Sidney was pleased – until he realized the third channel featured a man with a Yasser Arafat-type stubble-beard standing and fulminating against Sidney in front of a large letter A with a circle around it: the Anarchist symbol. Sidney sighed. He had some tough sledding ahead, he feared.

CHAPTER 9

On the TV the previous night, Sidney had learned that there would be two big demonstrations that day in Barcelona. One, organized by the communists, was to march west to east along the Gran Vía de les Corts Catalanes – in 1960 the Avenida de José Antonio Primo de Rivera, son of a former Spanish dictator and founder of the Falangist Party.

A second group of demonstrators was being mobilized by the Anarchists of Catalunya and would march from north to south along the Avenida Diagonal – in 1960 the Avenida del Generalísimo Francisco Franco – then south down the former Paseo de la Gracia, now, to Sidney, bastardized into some stupid Catalán version. Both marches would end up at the Plaza de Cataluña, the main square of Barcelona, at approximately one p.m.

The Plaza de Cataluña

Well! It didn't take a mental giant, Sidney mused, to reason that these two old enemy groups (although both had fought grudgingly on the same side – and each other – in the Spanish Civil War) would most likely not greet each other in friendship upon meeting at the Plaza de Cataluña. Indeed, a massive riot seemed inevitable. Why couldn't the authorities see this? Probably because each side had its supporters in the Generalitat, and neither would back down. Both parties argued over which had planned their march first.

Sidney figured that this was his chance to make two huge groups of angry people aware, possibly for the first time, that their courses (they both wanted independence for Cataluña) were self-destructive and would tear Spain apart. Nodding his head affirmatively, he went out of his hotel, Pancho in tow, to look for an art supply store.

He found one within two blocks of the Colón, and there he bought two large, sturdy pieces of white illustration board, a yardstick (meterstick?), a pencil, some tape and a very large black Magic Marker. Then he and Pancho returned to his hotel room and he began work, measuring and drawing lines, first with pencil, then with the large, black Magic Marker. When finally finished, he had a big, four-foot-by-six-foot white billboard with the old yoke and arrows symbol of the Catholic Kings Fernando and Isabel – also, though he paid no heed to Pancho's concern, the symbol adopted by the Falangist Party in the 1930s and which most people today read as *FRANCO*. The two boards were taped together, though the sign could fold in half for easier porterage. Now Sidney and a concerned-looking Pancho set out for the Plaza de Cataluña.

Two political platforms had been constructed in the plaza, one for each party, both with portable bullhorns for addressing the faithful – and the unfaithful. Sidney could hear the roar of the two approaching crowds as they surged, inexorably, toward the Plaza de Cataluña. Both were chanting slogans which, had they been in English, would have demonstrated some really deep thinking, Sidney told himself, such as their Catalán equivalents of:

Ho, ho, ho!

Spain's gotta go!

(Repeat 1000 times)

and

One, two, three, four!

Throw Spain out the door!

(Repeat 1000 – no, make that 2000 times)

Sidney, a professor of literature, thought to himself: *if one of my students came up with a chant that lame, I'd flunk him/her/it.*

When the two groups finally entered the square, Sidney got his first look at them. The Anarchists were led by an attractive yet fierce-looking, youngish woman with long, black hair pulled back severely, into a ponytail and wearing a sweatshirt with a circled letter A on the front. Sidney later learned that the woman's name was Satana Iglesia Quemada. Entering the plaza separately at first but inevitably mixing with the Anarchists as they progressed, were the communists, led by a fiftyish, hard-looking man called (as, again, Sidney learned later) *Camarada Titianio.* He wore a long, black leather coat and a black leather, peaked cap with a red star on it. Sidney thought, hmmm – Titanio, or Titanium in English; that's even tougher than steel – and steel is *Stalin* in Russian. Many in both groups wore coveralls and boiler suits and carried tire irons, big wrenches, etc.

Demonstrators marching to Plaza de Cataluña

Before either of the leaders could mount their platforms, Sidney and Pancho climbed up onto one of them. Pancho was told to hold up the big *Reyes Católicos* (and Franco) sign. Sidney had in the meantime confiscated a bullhorn from a kid in an Anarchist teeshirt who was apparently so blown away on weed that he actually said, "*Gracias,* man", when Sidney offered to hold it for him.

The two group leaders then saw Sidney, Pancho and the big sign on the platform. Especially the sign. Now, there were undoubtedly some *Barcelonistas* who would have applauded the sign, but not those present today. Both leaders started to yell in objection, but at that moment Sidney opened up with the bullhorn.

"People of Spain! F'rget the road to destruction thy leadeth'rs art taking thee down! Joineth together, once again, in a unit'd Spain!"

Well, most of the crowd couldn't hear what Sidney was saying, even with the bullhorn. But they could sure as hell see the big sign that Pancho was holding up and which, to them, said "Franco" or "Falangist Party". They began charging the platform, the most eager of the lot a mass of college-age student types who had been gathered in front of the Telefónica building on the west side of the plaza. Just as this lot of student types deserted the area where they had been gathered, in favor of an angry charge toward the speakers' platform, to get Sidney -- along with many of the marchers of both groups of demonstrators -- the sidewalk in front of the Telefónica erupted in a huge explosion, knocking many people down and sending others running for their lives in other directions. Cries of "Falangist bombs! Run!" filled the air. Even the Anarchist and Communist bosses fled the plaza, but each tried to be sure the other one was ahead in the process of fleeing. Sidney and Pancho were left standing alone on the platform, unsure of exactly what had happened.

That night the TV news *en castellano* (only one channel, the one everyone watched) revealed how a strange man speaking Medieval Spanish and claiming to be "el Cid" at the Generalitat the previous day, was responsible for the saving of many lives at the mass demonstration in the Plaza de Cataluña that afternoon, when he caused a group of youths to suddenly abandon the area where they had been loitering in front of the Telefónica, only seconds before a gas main exploded there. Several people had been injured, the anchorman said, but thanks to the man called "el Cid", who had, using a bullhorn, said something to make the youths leave their previous spot, dozens, maybe hundreds, of lives had been saved. "Cataluña owes much to 'el Cid'", the newsman said, a sort of half-smirk on his face.

CHAPTER 10

One of the greatest minds of Medieval Spanish Literature –
perhaps *the* greatest living mind on the subject in the
entire world – sat down with his worshipful manservant
in his room at the proud old Hotel Colón and began to
plot. He spread out a map of the country. "Ah, the Basque
state!" he said, as though discovering it. On his first trip
to Spain he had gone there. True, he had gone to San
Sebastián (now ridiculously called Donostía), not Vitoria,
but Pancho said Vitoria was the so-called capital of the
Basque country. And Pancho had told him that there
was a movement by some of the Basques to achieve full
independence from Spain. This tomfoolery must, like that
of Cataluña, be quashed before it got out of hand.

Sidney had heard of Vitoria. It was located inland from the coastal cities of Bilbao and San Sebastián. But somewhere along the way, somebody – obviously a Basque – had added a second, hyphenated name to the place. Now, apparently, it was called, at least by some people (including those who had made Sidney's map of Spain) Vitoria-Gasteiz. What kind of name was Gasteiz, for God's sake? Sidney knew the answer: a non-Spanish, non-traditionalist, Basque name, that's what. Sidney seethed. Well, call it Vitoria-Gas Station or whatever, Sid would ride Bibíeca there and – well, he would see.

The City of Vitoria

CHAPTER 11

Sidney decided to take the scenic route this time. After all, the *autopista* was just like driving an interstate back home, except that often you had to pay for it at toll booths. The countryside was nice along the old, two-lane highway; the problem was that there weren't any of those *autopista* rest stops/gas stations, and as he and Pancho were a few kilometers out of Vitoria, the Jeep started sputtering, then died. To his chagrin, Sidney glanced at the fuel gauge and saw the needle *below* empty. He was out of gas.

"*Carajo!*" groaned Pancho. "This is nowhere, *señor*, and we are in the middle of it!"

Sidney let the Jeep roll onto the shoulder of the road, and there he pulled up the hand brake. Oh, brother. What to do now? He looked about him, seeing farmland in all directions. But he did see an old stone well, and that gave him an idea.

"Pancho," he said, smiling, the proverbial light bulb coming on above his head. "I may beest a professeth'r of medieval Spanish, not physics, but coequal I knoweth yond oil floateth on top of wat'r. And gasoline is madeth from oil. And th're hast to beest a tiny did bit of gas left in the bottom of the tank, just below the intake valve. And yond well ov'r th're belike hast some wat'r at the bottom of 't!" He got out of the Jeep and headed toward the well.

Sure enough, there was an old bucket attached to a rope, and when the professor lowered it into the stygian darkness, he finally heard a splash. He then pulled the bucket back up, full of water. Muddy water, true, but still water. He untied the rope from the bucket and carried it over to the Jeep, where he poured half the contents into the fuel intake. He replaced the bucket on the edge of the well, returned to his trusty Bibieca and prepared to start the engine.

"But, *señor!*" said Pancho, concern showing in his face. "The car, he runs on gasoline, not water!"

"Aye, Pancho, but we art going to tryeth f'r a miracle!" He turned the key in the ignition. The motor ground and coughed, then quit. Sidney tried again, and this time the engine caught, although it backfired a couple of times. He "gunned it" and the roar was a bit steadier, though there were still backfires.

"This shall hopefully receiveth us into Vitoria," Sidney said, "and sure we can find a gas station there."

Pancho was dumbfounded. "It is a miracle!" he shouted. "You make the car run on water!" He looked at Sidney. "*Another* miracle! First water into wine, now this! You are truly el Cid Campeador, come to save Spain!"

They reentered the highway and continued at a slow pace on toward Vitoria. Another five minutes or so and they were nearing the outskirts, the Jeep continuing to backfire as they meandered along the winding road.

The city limits sign read, Vitoria-Gasteiz. Sidney muttered "Vitoria", omitting the add-on Basque name. Next to the sign was a placard displaying the city's official flag, which appeared to Sidney to be a duplicate of the Alabama state flag, a broad red X on a white field, except that the Basque version also had a small crest or coat of arms in the very center. To Sidney the crest looked like a pair of buzzards sitting atop the towers of a castle. "The buzzards belike no doubt representeth pro-independence traitors," Sidney said to Pancho, who replied. "*Si, señor.*"

Sidney had tuned into a local station over the Jeep's radio, and he was engrossed in a report of the exploits of Napoleon le Fou, a notorious French bank robber who had apparently been hitting banks throughout northeastern Spain, near France, in recent times. The police were, as the saying goes, baffled. What separated this crook from your run of the mill bank robber, it seemed, was that he always shouted out that "a sizeable portion" of his take would be going to ETX, the pro-independence Basque terrorist organization which supposedly "went out of business" in 2012, only to reappear the previous year, as times got worse all over Spain.

Pancho said ETX stood for Euskadi Ta Xskgtxui – Basque Home and Hearth. The political party associated with ETX was called Batapupu, and it claimed to represent all the Basque people in Spain in a quest for independence, although only about a quarter of the population of the Basque Country actually spoke the local language. Sidney suspected that le Fou actually gave little – if anything at all – to ETX or anybody else save himself, but he supposed that to some it may have sounded more noble to be championing a political agenda.

Sidney had been deep in thought and he almost missed the turnoff from the old highway onto the street that pointed to the center of Vitoria. He therefore made a wide turn, crossing over into the oncoming lane, the sudden erratic movement causing the Jeep to backfire several more times. Sounds like a gun battle, he thought.

At this moment, an oncoming car, an old, low-slung French Citroen which had been traveling at a high rate of speed, suddenly slewed sideways, its driver slamming on the brakes. With the Citroen now blocking the road, Sidney likewise slammed on his own brakes. The backfiring continued. What happened next left Sidney – and Pancho – speechless: the French car's front doors flew open and two men leaped out, their hands in the air. From further back down the road whence the Citroen had come, the ever-louder, hee-haw sound of a police car siren filled the air.

"Don't shoot!" cried the smaller of the two men in French, his arms outstretched above his head. "We give up! We thank *le bon Dieu* that you are lousy shots! All them shots, and not a single bullet hole in our car!" At that moment, a black bag fell out of the open passenger side door of the French car, spilling euro notes out into the street. Then, as the police car roared up and squealed to a stop behind the two fugitives, the smaller man yelled at Sidney and Pancho in heavily accented Spanish, mixed with a little French, "*Merde*! You guys ain't cops! And that Jeep ain't no Guardia Civil Land Rover! Dammit, Pierre! If they hadna been shootin' at us, I never woulda had us stop!"

Two policemen leaped from the car marked *Policía Local*, their pistols drawn and both of them yelling, *"Manos arriba!"* Gesturing hysterically, they shoved the two culprits into the back seat of the police car, then while one of them guarded the Frenchmen, the other scrambled around on the street, stuffing euro notes back into the black bag. When he had finished, he turned to Sidney and Pancho.

"Señores, mil gracias for helping us stop these bank robbers! The short one is the notorious Napoleon le Fou. You have done Spain a great service! Thanks to you, le Fou and his accomplice will soon be behind bars! If I may ask, *señores*, who do I have the honor of speaking with?"

Sidney spoke. "I am L. Sidney Camp, and this is mine own assistant, Pancho Zinsano."

"El Cid Campeador!" gasped the first policemen. "*Sí,* we have heard of you! You are returned, to save Spain!" He noted with approval Sidney's lapel pin.

"Get his autograph, Pepe!" called out the other cop, from his watch over the thieves in the back seat of the patrol car.

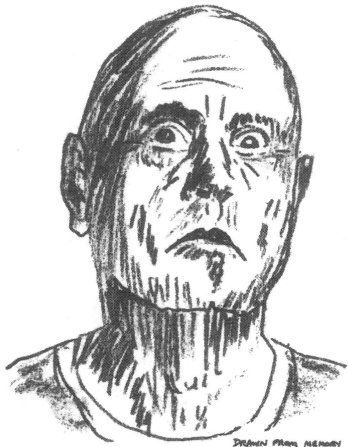

DRAWN FROM MEMORY
BY L. SID CAMP —
AFTER MY ADVENTURE

Napoleon le Fou

CHAPTER 12

That night Sidney and Pancho and their part in the capture of the French bank robber Napoleon le Fou and his crony led all the TV news programs. And to ensure that the thieves gained no sympathy from Basques, a spokesman for ETX appeared on television in shadow, bitterly refuting le Fou's claim that he had been donating to the Basque terrorist organization.

Reporters also related the recent encounter with the president of the Catalán Generalitat, emphasizing "el Cid's" quest for a reunited Spain. And one network had even learned about Sid's episode with the wind turbines in la Mancha. What started out as a tale of buffoonery soon became a *cause célèbre* when the envisioned great wind power project off Cape Trafalgar was related and Spaniards imagined tens of thousands of giant, white propellers on poles, completely encircling the entire coastline of their country. El Cid, it was said, had recognized this dire threat for what it actually was and had, in dramatic fashion, drawn the attention of the Spanish people and, indeed, the world, to the nefarious plot.

On TV, Sidney was thanked by the mayor of Vitoria, "for delivering Spain yet again from a Napoleonic scourge from the north." (Some nervous laughter here.) *El alcalde* then asked "the new Cid" if he could do anything for him, anything at all. Sidney struck whilst the iron was hot: Why, yes, he replied in his bizarre but understandable medieval Spanish, now that hizzoner mentioned it, he would very much like to meet the Basque president. The mayor sputtered a bit, but then said he felt sure such could be arranged. The ears of the massed reporters immediately pricked up, as they remembered or had learned about Sidney's impromptu meeting with the president of the Generalitat in Barcelona. They would be there, that was for sure!

And when that meeting did indeed take place the next day, it was most assuredly a grand affair. In front of the government building in Vitoria the police band played, the featured piece being Beethoven's Opus 91, "The Battle of Vitoria" or "Wellington's Victory." The Basque *lehendakari,* or president, Jesús Maria

Leizaologuipuzcoa, officially welcomed "the new Cid" to the Basque Autonomous Community and thanked him yet again for his invaluable aid in capturing the nefarious Napoleon le Fou and his lackey, in the process recovering all monies taken in the latest heist. Sidney was then introduced to the crowd, who cheered him lustily as he stepped up to the mass of microphones on the podium. He thanked the president and the assembled people, and the local as well as imported media types – then he got straight to the point.

"Anon, since I doth not speaketh the Basque language," he said, "I shall speak to thee in Castellano. Aye, tis an antiquat'd v'rsion of Castellano, 'r Spanish, since I am, aft'r all, a professeth'r of Medieval Spanish did light'rature. But I imagine not that speaking Spanish shall presenteth a problem h're, since I und'rstand yond only twenty-seven p'rcent of Basques actually speaketh yond language – while one hundr'd p'rcent of thee speaketh Spanish (laughter here). I heareth a lot of talk of speak of things Basque h're and wherefore not? We be in the Basque country, foresooth (more laughter). But alloweth me asketh thee something. At which hour yond most wondrous Basque conquistador Vasco Nuñez de Balboa discover'd the Pacific Ocean, what state's flag did that gent planteth in the sand of the beach? A Basque flag? Nay, mine own cater-cousins, that gent plant'd the flag of

Spain! Forsooth, that gent is known throughout the w'rld as the *Spanish* explor'r Balboa!

"And who is't doth the w'rld knoweth as the first sir to hest a ship circumnavigating the globe? The Portuguese mariner Fernando Magellan? Nay, yond hon'rable gentleman kicked the bucket en route, in the Philippines. Twast of course the Basque, Juan Sebastian Elcano, who is't accomplish'd the palmy deed und'r the flag of Spain!

"All ov'r the w'rld th're art institutions – orders, churches, univ'rsities bearing the fustian nameth of Loyola. Anon, Martin Ignacio de Loyola wast a Basque, but his w'rks and his h'ritage art known to the peoples of the earth as *Spanish.* Aye, that gent wast a most wondrous Basque, but that gent was eke a most wondrous Spaniard! And twast und'r the auspices of *Spain* yond his fame wast did spread worldwide!

"Thee ladies out th're all knoweth of Paco Rabanne. But I wouldst did yond thee knoweth that gent as the *Spaniard* Paco Rabanne, rather than as the Basque *parfumier* Paco Cuerva – Frank Crow!

"And at which hour one speaks of the fusty master Basque painter Ignacio Zuloaga, or the incomparable Basque musical composer Maurice Ravel and his immortal *Bolero,* 'r the most wondrous Basque philosopher Miguel de Unamuno, 'r the Basque Nobel laureate f'r literature, José Echegaray – again, I would did bet yond the ordinary thinkest first as *Spanish,* and then, if 't be true at all, as Basques. This is not to denigrate their Basqueness, but rather to emphasize yond they are all important parts which comprise, 'long with men and distaff of other areas of this most wondrous land, yond one magnificent entity we knoweth as . . . *Spain!*"

Perhaps unable to help themselves, the crowd broke out into a loud and sustained cheer. From somewhere, a red-yellow-and-red Spanish flag appeared, waving from a tall pole. The TV cameramen were busy, shooting videos of the spontaneous outburst. Sidney and Pancho both found themselves hoisted onto shoulders and carried through the streets to their hotel, as though they were triumphant bullfighters. The Basque president was left at the deserted podium, his mouth hanging open, as the police band boomed out the theme music from the 1961 movie, *El Cid.*

What Sidney was not aware of was the rough-looking bunch of fiercely independence-minded Basque nationalists in the crowd, all members of ETX, who were scowling, not smiling.

Sidney and Pancho finally got settled into their hotel and Sidney was laying out his things when he noticed a piece of paper being slid under his room's door. He

DRAWN FROM MEMORY
BY L. SID CAMP —
AFTER MY ADVENTURE

Police band, Vitoria

immediately crossed the room and opened the door, looking both ways down the hall, but whoever had delivered the note was already gone. Sidney opened the folded sheet of cheap, schoolchildren's lined paper with a penciled message written thereon in block letters complete with misspellings:

> *DO NOT THINK YOU WILL SUCCEED*
> *IN YOUR EVAL*
> *ATEMP TO CHANGE SPAIN BACK TO*
> *A MEDEVAL*
> *FASCIST STATE. WE WILL STOP YOU.*

There was no signature *per se*; instead, there were just the three letters, ETX.

CHAPTER 13

It was late afternoon now, and as he was relaxing in his "servant's quarters" room of the Hotel Altamira in Santillana del Mar – nicer than anything he had known in his pre-Cid days – Pancho was reflecting on how his life had changed over the past few days. He unabashedly worshipped the man he called el Cid Campeador. He knew in his heart that this fine man had been sent by God to save Spain in this, the dark time. People were out of work (as he had been), and the national economy had plummeted. Some still rankled over the loss in 1898 to the United States, at the end of the Spanish-American War, the last remnants of its once-great, globe-girdling empire. In various regions where some of the people spoke a dialect different from Castellano, a minority wanted to pull away from Spain and try to be independent. And now there were even rumors that Spain might be thrown out of the European Union and that His Majesty the King might abdicate – but in favor of who or what? El Cid, Pancho knew, would turn it all around. He would save Spain!

Curled up on his luxurious bed, Pancho fell asleep and dreamed – of el Cid charging the giant wind turbines in la Mancha, of el Cid forcing his way into the Generalitat in Barcelona and telling el presidente what he must do, of the miracles of el Cid turning water into wine, and water into motor car fuel, of el Cid's apprehension of the famous French bank robber Napoleon le Fou, of the great speech by el Cid to the Basques.

Yes, Pancho was a lucky man, he told himself. Why, in his last job, he had been working as a septic tank cleaner. Ugh! He had finally quit that horrible work but then had been unable to find any other employment. Things were tough in Spain. Until that lucky day in Madrid when he had met el Cid. Now, he knew, all would be all right – for him and for Spain. Why, without el Cid, would he ever, among other things, have come to Altamira?

This was of course where the world-famous Cave of Altamira was located, the incredible series of underground chambers whose walls and ceilings were decorated with cave paintings of hunters and their animal prey dating back more than 22,000 years. ("That was even before Franco, was it not, *señor*?" Pancho had asked.) The original cave had been open only to serious scholars for years, and the Spanish government had created a duplicate cave and copies of all the paintings virtually next door, and tourists could visit this faux site. Happily, the original cave was once again open to the public, on a limited basis, and Sidney had reserved an entrance in advance, through the good offices of his university.

So, prior to a planned visit to nearby Santander on the north coast of Spain – as elegant as anything on the French Riviera, many people said – Sidney and Pancho had driven to the prize of the province of Cantabria, Santillana del Mar. As they arrived late in the day, after the cave museum had closed, they checked into the sixteenth century Hotel Santillana and looked forward to the morrow.

DRAWN FROM MEMORY
BY L. SID CAMP —
AFTER MY ADVENTURE

Cave paintings, Altamira

CHAPTER 14

Sidney sat at the antique desk in his room, partaking of the complimentary half bottle of wine which was a gift from the hotel management. Like all Spanish wines, it was better than its world image. The ageing professor with the bushy head of gray hair sipped and mused over the changes which had taken place in Spain since his last visit in 1960. Now, instead of the rickety old rail coaches pulled by a coal-burning, smoke-billowing locomotive, there was the AVE, the sleek Alta Velocidad Española, with speeds up to more than 190 miles per hour. And highways clogged with privately owned automobiles, not just foul-smelling, lumbering, diesel trucks grinding their way along. The people were taller now, especially the young people; better diet, no doubt. And the women no longer wore the predominately black dresses of widows or other female relatives of a lost loved one – even if it happened years ago. The monied ladies were now all streaked blondes, the rest still brunettes.

There were no more paraplegics from the 1936-39 war – perhaps holding a job as a train or bus conductor or a parking lot attendant. Shoeshines were then three cents U.S. while recently a vile robber had tried to charge him nine euros for one.

On his first trip, Sidney had brought a camera with him, along with a package of flash bulbs – which in those days were a requirement for making photographs in low light. When he entered Spain by train in 1960, it was via Irun, opposite St. Jean de Luz, just across the border in France. When the usual bag inspection took place in the small, white stucco building on the Spanish side used by *la aduana español*, the Guardia Civil man in his patent leather hat with the back brim turned up began going through Sidney's things, and he came across the flash bulbs. With great alarm he pulled out the package and held it up for all to see.

"Bombas!" he cried, triumphantly. Perhaps he would get a promotion for discovering a Red planning on terrorism in Spain.

Sidney tried to explain to the man that these were just flash bulbs *para sacar fotografias*, but the Civil Guard was not even listening. He was too busy showing his *compañeros* what he had uncovered. Finally, Sidney had fit one of the flashbulbs onto his camera and snapped a flash photograph of the *guardia*, who was so startled he went for his sidearm, but his colleagues burst out laughing. Humiliated, the guard ordered Sidney to get out – now. And take his damned flash bulbs with him. Ah, the flash bulb saga.

There did not seem to be any talk about Reds any more; everybody said back then that there was probably a Red behind every tree, but the young Sidney had checked behind quite a few trees, before giving up the hunt. They were just hard to actually catch on the job, the youth surmised.

Sidney sipped his wine. Now, wine was certainly a different story, as well. He remembered paying the equivalent of ten cents U.S. for a decent bottle of table wine. Well, truth be told, he remembered a *friend* buying the wine – in those days, as a young and sheltered student, Sidney did not drink anything alcoholic. Indeed, he recalled an incident in Pamplona in 1960 when he and an American friend had found themselves seated at a table with three Spanish workers from Jaen, in town for the *sanfermines* and the running of the bulls through the streets. Though obviously poor, the Spaniards had ordered a jug of wine and now offered some to their new American friends. The jug had a little spout on the top, and the idea was to hold it out at arm's length and pour a stream of wine into one's mouth – hopefully without pouring part of it onto one's shirt. But when it came time for Sidney to chug his portion, the nineteen-year old lad tried to politely decline, explaining that he didn't drink wine. Well! This made about as much sense to the three workers from Jaen as if Sid had said he didn't drink *water.* They all frowned and looked at each other. Was this foreigner committing an insult? Was their wine not good enough? One of the men actually began rising from his chair, scowling, fiercely, when Sid's American friend hissed at him in English, "For God's sake, Sid, drink some of that wine, or at least pretend to drink some! Otherwise, they're probably going to break that jug over your head!" So Sid held he spout up to his lips as he would a bottle, and pretended to drink, then passed the jug to his friend. The Spaniard slowly sat back down, and all three smiled. Crisis over.

Nowadays, of course, Sid enjoyed a good wine. His favorite Spanish vintage was Teso la Monja. However, as this particular wine cost approximately $1,041.00 U.S. per bottle at home, he rarely enjoyed it. More accurately, he had never actually tasted it, but at $1,041.00 U.S. a bottle, surely it *had* to be good. He had not, he reflected, tried the new, blue-colored Spanish wine called *Gik*. Sid could of course "go slumming" in his wine searches, just for fun. For example, he often purchased the American bulk process champagne André, at $3.99 a bottle.

Sid felt a lump in his pants pocket and pulled out a red "cherry bomb" a little smaller than a golf ball. Well, at least that hadn't changed. The firecracker, jokingly given to him by Pancho after a stop at a service station en route, was one of the millions still produced in Valencia, the fireworks capital of Europe and maybe the world. He didn't really want the thing, but what to do with it? He put it back in his pocket.

Yes, Spain had otherwise changed in many ways, a few of them, Sidney ruefully admitted to himself, for the better. But, all in all, he was sure that Spain during the period of the eleventh through the fifteenth centuries was the model to strive for. The period of el Cid!

The two men enjoyed a good meal and some nice but not overpriced wine in the hotel dining room, amid medieval trappings. They would get a good night's sleep, then proceed to the famous cave, a short walk from the hotel, in the morning. But first, Sidney suggested, why not take that short walk now, before going to bed, and just see what the cave looked like from the outside? Pancho of course agreed.

When they were at the entrance of the cave, now closed for the day to the public, several men – perhaps eight or ten – were standing around a small wood fire, all of them looking menacing. A brown-bearded fellow stepped forward.

"You two, there! Stop!" he said. Sidney and Pancho did as they were told, looking around to note that no one else was in the vicinity, not even a guard or night watchman. They were alone with these dubious-looking men in workers' clothing, in front of the ticket booth and entrance turnstile.

The apparent leader of the group, a short, stocky man, the one with a brown beard, said, "We know of your plan to dismantle the Cave of Altamira and ship it to the United States!" he shouted. "And the fake cave for tourists with it!"

Stunned, Sidney could only blubber, "What?"

"Do not play the innocent with me!" shouted the man. "Admit it!"

"And where in the United States art we did suppose to beest shipping the anters to?" Sidney asked, calmly.

"What? Anters? Oh, you mean caves. Well, uh,

to Disney World in Florida, of course," shot back the bearded man.

Sidney laughed. "Yond is ridiculous! Where on earth didst thee receiveth yond idea? And wherefore me? I am but a college professeth'r!"

"Do not lie to us!" cried the man. "We of all people know what you foreigners have planned to do to poor Cantabria! You, the would-be Cid, and your cronies from America! And we, the PCC – the Partido de Chalados de Cantabria to you – are going to prevent it!"

"The PCC?" queried Sidney. "And I presume yond then, liketh the Catalans and the Basques, has't a language of thy owneth and thee wanteth to beest idependent of Spain, right?"

"Of course we have our own language!" shot back the Cantabrian. "And a full three thousand people speak it! Maybe more! The people properly known as the *Montañés* – those from the mountain! Yes, we want to be independent! And we mean to prevent any outsiders having our caves!"

"Oh, aye," said Sidney. "The Cantabrian dialect. *Montañés.*"

"It is *not* a dialect!" screamed the man. "It is a proper *language*! The language of an independent country of six hundred thousand people!"

Sidney paused, obviously thinking, then said, "One half of one percent of whom speaketh this so-call'd language."

"It is still our language!" yelled the bearded one. "And the caves are ours as well! They are either ours or nobody's!"

Sidney smiled. "And just how were Pancho and I to dismantle these anters and ship those folk to Florida?"

"Never mind how!" bellowed the man. "No doubt some Yankee machinery is on its way here now, by ship – or by truck! But we know how to foil your evil plan! We are going to fix it so that the caves and their paintings that are of such great interest to capitalist entrepreneurs cannot be shipped to anyplace! Because we are unionized Cantabrian miners with a knowledge of dynamite! We are going to blow up the caves – with you and your friend inside them! If we can't have the caves, *nobody* will!" One of the group of men smilingly held forth a bundle of dynamite sticks with a fuse dangling down its side.

The bearded man spoke wildly again. "Disney World!

A ridiculous capitalistic enterprise for the idle rich! And those cave paintings, all done by non-union hunters and artists! Pre-capitalists! All of them!" Foam was actually coming out of the corners of his mouth.

Sidney had been standing with his back to the fire, and his hands in his pants pockets. Slowly, he grasped the cherry bomb given to him earlier by the *valenciano* Pancho and withdrew it from his pocket; just as the bearded PCC man screamed his last words about the ancient cave painters being pre-capitalists, his hands waving in the air, Sidney unobtrusively flipped the firecracker into the small bonfire behind his back. It exploded instantly with a very loud bang, showering the area, including all the men, good and bad, with sparks and small glowing embers.

"Police!" cried Sidney, "Run!"

Suddenly the entire area in front of the caves was bathed in brilliant artificial light from floodlights mounted around the cave entrance, and a police-like siren began wailing, incredibly loudly, automatically initiated by the explosion. A museum guard poked his head around a now-opened doorway leading into the main cave. In his navy blue uniform, he looked like a policeman.

"Run!" yelled the bearded man, instantly forgetting about Sidney and Pancho. The other men in his group needed no prodding: they all bolted like horses fleeing a burning barn. Within seconds, all of them had disappeared into the night, leaving Sidney and Pancho in front of the cave entrance.

The museum guard, a man of perhaps sixty years, now approached, brandishing a pistol. He was obviously terrified, his gun shaking uncontrollably. "I heard it all!" he cried, his voice barely audible over the siren's continuing blast. "They were going to blow up the caves! With the two of you inside! The alarm will have alerted the police! They will be here shortly! Those men – they were PCC!"

"Can thee turneth off yond alarm?" Sidney asked the guard over the screeching noise and carefully pushing the barrel of the guard's pistol to one side, away from himself and Pancho. The guard looked at him as though in a daze, then seemed to "wake up", whereupon he nodded and went back into the cave. A moment later, the siren mercifully stopped, but the bright lights remained on. In the distance could be heard yet another siren, this time from an approaching police car.

DRAWN FROM MEMORY
BY L. SID CAMP —
AFTER MY ADVENTURE

Sidney's cherry bomb

CHAPTER 15

The professor and his sidekick had to tell their story twice, first, that night, to the police, and the next morning to the now-alerted media vultures who descended upon their hotel at dawn. The cave's night watchman had told first the local minions of the law and, later, the reporters – who began arriving before his shift was over at eight – all about how the two foreigners *[sic]* had foiled the plans of the PCC men to blow up the caves, putatively to prevent their being dismantled and carted off to Disney World in Florida. While none of the media reps gave any credence to the Disney World tale, they did display interest in the night watchman's description of the dynamite displayed by the would-be cave wreckers. And all had already heard of the new Cid and his quest to "save" Spain.

DRAWN FROM MEMORY
BY L. SID CAMP —
AFTER MY ADVENTURE

The media interviews Sidney

Pancho was thoroughly enjoying himself, explaining how he, in his infinite wisdom and with great foresight, had in advance supplied his friend *el señor* el Cid Campeador with a most powerful *petardo de Valencia* for use in just such a case as this. Then he went on to extol the fame and quality of the pyrotechnics produced in Valencia, the fireworks capital of the entire world. The men and women of the media, however, showed little interest in the Valencia angle, though they did pepper Sidney with questions as to how he happened to be "armed" with a powerful firework when he encountered the PCC men.

Later, when everything had become quiet again, Sidney visited the original Cave of Altamira. And as the hero of the day, they even permitted Pancho to accompany him inside at no charge. Both men – but particularly Sidney – were agog at the fantastic wall and ceiling drawings and paintings in red, ochre, black and shades of yellow, many of them life-sized. Pancho exhaled and exclaimed quite a bit, and he once asked Sidney, "*Señor*, why did these hunters not use rifles? That would have been much easier than bows and arrows and spears!" Sidney just shrugged and went on with his admiration.

That evening the news on television was full of the story of the now-famous "new Cid" and his saving of the Cave of Altamira at the hands – and bundles of dynamite – of a group of men identified by the night watchman as members of the PCC. There were video clips and photos of "el Cid Campeador" of the USA and his Spanish friend Pancho Zinsano, from Valencia. Sidney and Pancho were truly household names now.

CHAPTER 16

Sidney had ensconced himself and Pancho in Santiago de Compostela's most fabulous hotel, el Hostal de los Reyes Católicos, a huge building in the Baroque and Plateresque styles opposite the cathedral, in the center of the city, and positively reeking with history. Constructed by "the Catholic Kings" Fernando and Isabel in 1486 as a hospice and hospital for pilgrims completing the long pilgrimage trail from Central Europe to the burial site of St. James, or Santiago, it was now a five-star-deluxe hotel which has been called "the most beautiful hotel in Europe". Why on earth had he tried to duplicate the days of his youth on his first stay in Madrid by using that awful Pensión Camel Dung?

Sidney wanted to continue his quest to do what he

could to get Spain "back on the right track," but he also wanted to see some parts of the country he had missed in 1960. Hence this visit to Santiago, in the far northwest of the Iberian Peninsula, the end of the line for pilgrims with their characteristic long walking sticks, and the site of the great Cathedral of Santiago de Compostela, celebrated as the burial place of the original St. James of the Twelve Apostles, and known also for its Chapel of the Reliquary containing a gold crucifix dating back to 874, as well as an alleged piece of the True Cross. It was also said that the massive church would have been the repository of yet another mind-boggling inclusion, had this last item not been lost at sea in the nineteenth century.

As the story went, a Mexican Indian sculptor had, using pure solid silver mined near Taxco, created a fabulous Madonna and Child some two feet in height weighing one hundred forty kilos (over three hundred pounds), and known as *la Virgen y Niño con Pistola*, so named because the artist had placed in a tiny hand of the Baby Jesus, the Prince of Peace, a small replica of a Colt Peacemaker pistol, model 1876, brand new at the time – "to help him keep the peace." Regrettably, mother and child had been lost in a shipwreck during a storm off the Galician coast in 1877, during the reign of King Alfonso XII "the Peacemaker".

Hotel de los Reyes Católicos, Santiago de Compostela

A distraught King sought to have the relic replaced – if such were possible – and in fact a silver reliquary fashioned by José Losada was placed in the church's crypt in 1886. But the loss of *la Virgen y Niño con Pistola* was nevertheless sorely missed. Sidney regretted not being able to cast his eyes upon it.

He and Pancho had departed Santillana at dawn, fearful that otherwise they might well be hounded and followed by reporters seeking more news of "the new Cid". Now, after having driven to Santiago, which seemed far enough from Santillana to be safe and after getting settled into the hotel, Sidney reached for his bedside telephone.

Pancho was awakened by the ringing of his phone. He lifted the receiver, still sleepy after dozing since he and Sidney had checked in a couple of hours earlier.

"*Sí?*"

"Pancho? Sid here. Didst I waketh thee?"

"Oh, no, no, *Señor* el Cid! I was just, er –" His stomach rumbled; it was late afternoon now – time for a tapa or two.

"Never mind, Pancho. We has't some planning to

doth! Meeteth me in the lobby in, alloweth us sayeth, ten minutes."

"*Sí, señor!*" Pancho hung up the phone and rolled off the bed. Such luxury he had never before seen. Even though his room was a "servant's room", it had a medium-sized, flat-screen TV, a little refrigerator, a telephone and a thermostat. *Caramba*! Traveling with *Señor* el Cid certainly had its benefits. Pancho left the room and headed for the elevators.

In the plush lobby of the hotel Pancho chose one of two chairs facing a small table and waited on el Cid to show. Glancing around, he noticed a rough-looking, gray-bearded type sitting in a corner, reading a copy of a newspaper whose masthead read, the *Clarion of Independence*. The man looked at Pancho, then back to his newspaper.

In a couple of minutes Sidney walked out of an elevator and over to where Pancho was, the latter leaping to his feet like an automaton.

"Sitteth down, Pancho, prithee," said Sidney. The bearded man in the corner glared furiously. Sidney spread a map of Spain out on the table and began to talk to Pancho. After a few minutes, the two men rose from their chairs and headed for the hotel's main entrance. The bearded man folded his flimsy newspaper, put it in a pants back pocket, and followed the other two out of the hotel. The sun was starting to go down.

Sidney had parked his Jeep on the street half a block from the hotel, so the entourage of Sidney and Pancho and, a few steps behind, the bearded man, who now was speaking into a cell phone, paraded down the sidewalk. In a couple of minutes Sidney and Pancho were at the Jeep, but as they prepared to get in, two more bearded men appeared at their sides, pistols held at waist level.

"Get in the car, *señores!*" ordered the gray-bearded man from the hotel, who now also brandished a pistol. His gray beard contrasted with those of his companions: one with a brown beard, and the other with one of jet black. The pistols, however, were all black and evil-looking. Pancho looked for guidance at Sidney, who nodded: do what they say. Two of the men, including Gray Beard, climbed into the Jeep, Sidney and Pancho in the back, Gray Beard at the wheel. Black Beard, in the front passenger seat, turned to face his prisoners, pistol leveled. Gray Beard got the keys from Sidney, started the Jeep and pulled away from the curb and into the flow of traffic. Brown Beard followed in another car. When they were in the back streets of Santiago, Black Beard, still with his pistol pointing threateningly, produced two blindfolds and instructed Sidney and Pancho to put them on, which they did. They then drove for perhaps half an hour, some of it twisting and turning through city streets, but the last part apparently in the country. Eventually they drove over a bumpy, unpaved track, then stopped and the blindfolds were removed. It was dark now, and they could smell the sea. They were in what appeared to be an old stone-walled carriage house – with a stone ceiling but without windows. Their abductors' flashlights lit the area after the Jeep's headlights were turned off.

"Get out!" ordered Gray Beard. They did, and Black Beard fixed their hands behind their backs with some sort of plastic handcuffs. Brown Beard drove up and joined them. Sidney and Pancho were pushed through an arched stone doorway and began climbing a seemingly endless spiral stone staircase, occasionally passing landings onto which closed, oaken and iron-studded doorways faced. All light was from the abductors' flashlights.

At last they came to yet another strong oaken door, and Gray Beard unlocked it with a massive, old-fashioned key. Sidney and Pancho were pushed inside, then the others followed. The two captives were ordered to sit on the stone floor, their backs to the circular stone wall. Their hand bindings now were removed. High up, there was one open, glassless window about a foot square; the sky outside was dark. The sound of waves crashing could be heard through the window. They were obviously in a tower room of an ancient castle – the top room, since the winding staircase had ended at the door. To Sidney, it sounded as though the three men were speaking Portuguese to each other.

"Ah!" said Sidney. "*Voce fala Portugues!*"

"No!" bellowed Gray Beard. "*Not* Portuguese! Galician!"

"But has't not scholars declared Galician to beest but a slightly did modify Portuguese? Just minor changes?"

Gray Beard first said "What?" and then went apoplectic. "No!" he screamed. "No! Galician is a language of its own! And it is spoken by the Galician people!"

"Some of those folk, aye, I shall concede yond," replied Sidney. "But I has't read yond *all* of those folk speaketh Castellano. And what doth thee wanteth, concluded be it? A dram tiny second Portugal? Or doth thee just wanteth to beest another parteth of Portugal?"

"I will kill you!" cried Gray Beard, diving for Sidney with outstretched arms and grasping fingers. The other two men quickly restrained him, cautioning him that, after all, they did need the professor. Gray Beard backed off and calmed down.

DRAWN FROM MEMORY
BY L. SJ3 CAMP —
AFTER MY ADVENTURE

The abandoned castle in Galicia

"All right, you Franco fascist pig, I will tell you," he said. "I see your Falange Party badge" – he pointed to Sidney's lapel pin – so I know where *you* stand! But we, the people for an independent Galicia, we stand for something different!" He yanked off Sidney's lapel pin and threw it out the high window.

"Liketh what?" Sidney asked.

"Like an Iberian Peninsula made up of independent states, each speaking its own language and free of capitalism and servitude to Spain, the European Union and the United States! We are the movement known as los Malucos Galegos!"

Sidney rolled his eyes. "A worker's Elsium – Toweth'r of Babel style," he said, now shaking his head in pity.

"Yes!" Exactly!" cried Gray Beard. "You can laugh, but it will happen!"

Pancho plucked at Sidney's sleeve. "*Señor*, is that where we are, then? Are we in the Tower of Babel? I seem to have heard of it."

"I shall pray pardon me later, Pancho," Sidney said, patting his friend's arm.

"And you can forget escape from this tower, fascist

pigs," said Gray Beard." You have a small open window, *si*, but we are fifteen meters off the ground, and the wall is sheer. After a few days without food you will be happy to appear on Galician television and recant your insane quest! And that will be the end of the new Cid's colorful attempt to reestablish a Medieval Spain! You see, no one – and I mean no one – lives on this rock-bound promontory facing the *Oceano Atlántico*. This ruined castle has been abandoned since 1740. The only people ever coming to this area are the occasional shepherds, and they leave this castle alone, as it is said to be haunted!" The Malucoman laughed maniacally, then said something in Portuguese – at least it sounded like Portuguese to Sidney – to his two accomplices, who started toward the low, iron-bound door.

"We will be back – in a few days. We will expect a changed man! He laughed again, and the three men exited the round tower room, locking the ancient door behind them. Their footsteps clattered down the circular stone staircases.

CHAPTER 17

Sidney looked around the room, including the tiny foot-square, glassless window some ten feet off the stone floor. Closer to the floor, below the window, an iron ring was set into the wall, probably to chain someone to it, in the past. "Pancho, maketh a stirrup with thy hands and boost me up to yond window." Pancho did as he was told, and in a moment the professor was gazing out the window, his elbows braced on the bottom of the aperture. In the moonlight he saw that they were indeed on a high, rocky promontory jutting out into the Atlantic. Sparse grass grew in the rock-strewn ground. No buildings could be seen. The sea looked rough, and the sky was partly cloudy. A stiff wind was blowing. Sidney told Pancho what he saw, then eased himself back to the stone floor.

"What do we do now, *señor*?" Pancho asked, turning his hat in his hands.

"Pancho, we doth what men has't done through the centuries at which hour did imprison falsely. We writeth a Spanish Prisoner Letter!"

"A Spanish Prisoner Letter?"

"Aye, We pray pardon me our situation and where we art, throweth the letter out the window and desires someone finds t, reads t, and then helps us!"

"But, but, *señor*, there is no one around to find such a letter and to read it!"

"Well, Pancho, yond is the way tis done in the romantic novels. And tis what we shall tryeth! At least yond is what we shall doth at which hour tis lighteth enow to seeth."

"*Si, señor.*"

"I of course might not but locateth a piece of paper on which to writeth mine own letter. Ah! In mine own pocket I feeleth a rather lengthy credit card chargeth slipeth from the hotel! The backeth side of t'will doth nicely, and I of course at each moment carryeth a ballpoint pen in mine own pocket."

"Of course."

When the sky finally lightened after a long, sleepless night, Sidney put the piece of paper on the smoothest stone he could find in the floor, and began to write. At last he was finished, and he read the message aloud to Pancho:

"I has't headed t, '*A Spanish Prison'r Lett'r.*' T reads, '*Help! 'long with a cousin, I am a prison'r in the toweth'r cubiculo of an masterless castle on a headland ov'rlooking the Atlantic Ocean. There is an ope window, but tis some fifteen hath meter high up. We wouldst normally attempteth to escapeth by tying bedsheets togeth'r but we has't nay bedsheets. Did fold with this message fifty euros noteth. Prithee purchaseth'r otherwise secureth a rope'r sev'ral bedsheets a total of at least fifteen hath meters in length and bringeth those folk to our toweth'r window. Thy reward shall beest one hundr'd euros. Signed, The Spanish Prison'r, eke known as el Cid'*.'"

Pancho had a safety pin holding together a rip in his trousers, and Sidney borrowed it to pin the fifty euro note to the scrawled message and therefore immediately make the missive more important-looking. He then folded the original message into the long triangular shape of a paper airplane and sailed it out the window. The wind caught it and carried it aloft for some distance; then it leveled off and headed toward a distant pasture.

CHAPTER 18

About a half mile away, a young shepherd named Diego was sleeping on the grass in the early morning, his small flock of sheep all nearby, pulling up the green shoots by the roots. Sidney's paper plane message landed point first in the snoring shepherd's open mouth, waking him from his slumber. He swatted at his face, extracting the paper missile and the attached fifty euro bill. Although Diego could neither read nor write, he knew full well what a fifty euro note was, and he unfolded it with great excitement. He puzzled over the handwritten message for a few moments, then got to his feet. He would go to the nearby Iglesia de Nuestra Señora de la Noche and ask Padre Culorero what the writing meant. It might be important. He began driving his sheep in the direction of the little church not too far away.

DRAWN FROM MEMORY
BY L. SID CAMP —
AFTER MY ADVENTURE

Diego the young shepherd

Diego eventually found Padre Culerero leading a young altar boy into his small house behind the church, preparatory to an early nap. The shepherd hailed the priest, who seemed a bit put out at the interruption in his schedule, but the sacerdote did reluctantly read aloud the handwritten message shown to him. Diego had kept the fifty euro note.

"Rope?" asked the priest. "Who has so much rope? Or bedsheets, for that matter." Diego could not answer that. He had neither; he slept on the dirt floor of his humble hut. Then, suddenly, he smiled broadly.

"I know, *padre*!" exclaimed the shepherd. "The big store in the town. El Corte Inglés! Sheets, anyway!" And before Padre Culorero could reply, Diego was running off, driving his small flock of sheep before him.

DRAWN FROM MEMORY
BY L. SUS CAMP —
AFTER MY ADVENTURE

Padre Culorero

CHAPTER 19

While Diego was hurrying off in search of the Housewares Department in the big store, el Corte Inglés, in the nearest town of any size, Corcubión, Sidney was looking carefully at the inner walls of his stone tower prison. Upon close examination, he could see many scratchings in the stone – some words, some basic drawings, some indecipherable markings. The most recent date he could find was 1898, so if the castle really had not been lived in for as long as the Maluco man had said, it had nevertheless apparently been used, probably as a prison, in more modern times.

One inscription was in Latin and was puzzling to Sidney until he figured it out. Scratched in the surface of the stone were the words, *Pacificator summo diluculo qui quaerit ut incipiat – He who seeks the peacemaker should begin at the top.* The peacemaker. Could this possibly refer to King Alfonso XII, the Peacemaker? Or – God in heaven – could it mean the small silver likeness of the *pistola*, the Peacemaker, said to be held in the hand of the little Prince of Peace, he of the lost *Virgen y Niño con Pistola?*

"Pancho!" he cried, waking his friend, who had gone back to dozing in a sitting position against the wall. "Crouch down! I neede to standeth on thy shouldst'rs!" Groggily, Pancho complied, and Sidney used his friend's shoulders as a stepladder. "Anon standeth up! I wanteth to examineth the top portion of this circular mure." Pancho groaned and shakily stood up.

Sidney spent several minutes atop poor Pancho, who stoically bore his master's weight with only the occasional groan. Of particular interest to the professor were the joints between the stones composing the wall. Each block was roughly a foot square, and Sidney seemed to be concentrating on the vertical cracks between the individual stones. At length he found something.

"Eureka!" he cried, then proceeding to prod one particular crack with the blade of his tiny keychain penknife. Eventually he gingerly extracted a folded piece of parchment-like paper.

"Down, Pancho!" he commanded, and he was momentarily standing once again on the floor, the paper in his hand. He unfolded it carefully, noting its brittle, crumbling state. There was pencil writing in Castellano on it, and he read:

The Testament of Julio Obregón e da Silva, 20 November 1877.

I was the navigator and, so far as I know, the only survivor of the good ship Estrella del Sur, *bound from Vera Cruz to Vigo with the pure silver reliquary* la Virgen y Niño con Pistola, *meant for the Cathedral of Santiago de Compostela as a gift from His Majesty Alfonso XII's still-loyal subjects in the former colony of México. Just off the coast of Finisterre, battered by gale force winds and mountainous seas, the ship went down at a point 9.35 west longitude and 46.85 north latitude, on the western side of the tiny Rocas de Guano, which are two rocks snow white with bird shit. Ships tend to steer clear of the rocks, and no humans go there since, as the name implies, they are covered with bird droppings. I crawled up onto the nasty rocks and two days later I was found and rescued by a* costa guarda *patrol boat.*

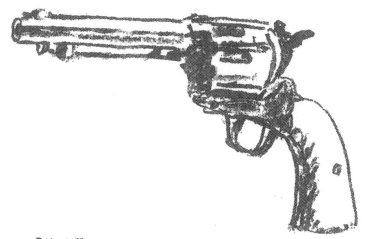

DRAWN FROM MEMORY
BY L. SID CAMP ——
AFTER MY ADVENTURE

A silver Colt Peacemaker

But upon being landed on the shore and telling my story to the local guardia civil, *I was taken away and locked into this tower room of what is apparently a disused castle. After much thought on the matter, I decided that someone here on the mainland – no doubt someone with a certain amount of authority – wants to keep the secret of the resting place of* la Virgen y Niño con Pistola *for selfish reasons, in order to salvage it for themselves. What they do not know is that I did not give them the correct and exact location of the wreck, so if I can escape from this place I plan to go to the true authorities of the church, or to the king himself if need be, in order to see the holy relic recovered and delivered to the Cathedral of Santiago de Compostela. If you hear no more of the reliquary, then I will have met an untimely fate.*

I am an educated man who wants not the reliquary for himself, but only to see that it goes where it was meant; I hope I am successful, but I fear my captors may do away with me.

(signed) Julio Obregón e da Silva

"Well, I am damned!" said Sidney.

CHAPTER 20

It was late morning when Sidney and Pancho heard a faint voice through the high window.

"*Señor!* It is I, Diego! Come to the window, please!"

Once again with Pancho's help, Sidney was looking out of the small, glassless window, his elbows on the stone sill. Far below, he could see the shepherd and his small flock of sheep. At his feet were several multicolored, flattish packages, apparently wrapped in clear plastic. Diego had one of them in his hands.

"Are you a ghost, *señor*?" shouted the shepherd.

"Nay! We beest flesh and blood!"

"Well, then, *señor*, catch!" he called out, and, with an underhand throw, he sailed the package end over end, up toward the window. It fell far short. Diego retrieved the package and tried again. And again. Finally, on about the seventh try, Sidney managed to catch it. He looked at a plastic-wrapped package about a foot square and perhaps two inches thick. The label read, *Superior Double Bed Sheets, top and bottom, non-fitted*. They were off-white, decorated with a wild floral print of pink, yellow and pale blue flowers. A sticker showed they had come from the store El Corte Inglés. Sidney tore open the package and pulled out the two sheets and two pillowcases, tossing the latter to the floor. The sheets were full sized. Enough of them would do the job. From below, Diego called back to him.

"I have more, *señor*!" And he began lofting the packages up to the little window. It took almost an hour, but at last Sidney had all seven packages of sheets. Then he got down off an exhausted Pancho and they began opening the packages, taking out the sheets, and making a long rope ladder of them, tied end to end.

Sidney tied one end to the iron ring set into the wall, and pitched the other end out the window. He then had Pancho go first, boosting him up to the little window, where he turned around awkwardly and then went out the window feet-first, on his stomach, lowering himself down the rope of sheets. Next, using the iron ring as a step, Sidney repeated the exercise, and eventually he was on the ground with Pancho and the shepherd – and with Obregón e da Silva's treasure map-letter in his pocket.

"Alloweth us receiveth out of here before those Maluco men returneth!" Sidney urged.

"But, *señor!*" said Diego. "My one hundred euros – please!"

Sidney sighed, and withdrew a C-note from his wallet, handing it to the smiling shepherd.

"*Anon* alloweth us wend!" And they did indeed leave, following Diego.

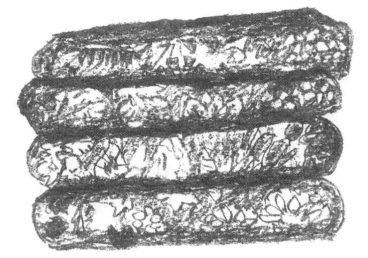

DRAWN FROM MEMORY
BY L. SID CAMP —
AFTER MY ADVENTURE

Packages of flowered bedsheets

CHAPTER 21

Sidney's main interest was in getting away from the deserted castle before the Maluco men returned. After that, he wanted to find someone with a goodsized fishing boat and deepsea diving equipment, for searching for the sunken ship with *la Virgen y Niño con Pistola*. Diego said he thought he knew a man with such a boat in the port city of Corcubión, the same city, he said, where he had "borrowed" the sheets from el Corte Inglés. He said this was some sixty kilometers west of Santiago de Compostela and less than ten kilometers from the town and peninsula named Finisterre ("end of the earth"), or Fisterra in Portuguese. The Portuguese border was about a hundred kilometers to the south as the crow – or the seagull – flew. From the old castle they had gotten Babieca the Jeep out of its barn-like, ground floor space originally meant for carriages – the keys were still in the ignition – and drove the fifteen or so kilometers to Corcubión, using the four-wheel-drive and traveling over the hilly inland, rather than the road, in order to avoid possibly meeting the Maluco men returning via the narrow dirt road.

In the port, Diego led them to the small harbor and a medium-sized fishing boat with a somewhat suspect motor, captained by one Juan el Pescador, who had aboard his vessel some scuba gear, though not any actual divers' suits with air hoses.

"Those gents shouldst suffice," said Sidney of the equipment, and, after an hour or so scrounging up a crew of three others, including a superannuated old fellow called Anselmo, and after agreeing on a price, they set off for las Rocas de Guano, fourteen kilometers to the west. Captain Juan said he knew the rocks well. Sidney had given Diego taxi fare to get back to his sheep.

In an hour, no more, they were at the rocks, white as snow, just as Obregón e da Silva had written in 1877. They putt-putted around to the west side, Sidney watching the sea bottom as best he could. The captain had a sextant, and when he told Sidney they were where they were supposed to be, they broke out the scuba gear.

Sidney had been a team swimmer in college, and he had done some scuba diving on vacations in the Caribbean, so he knew what to do, as did two of the crew, including old Anselmo. Sidney told them to look for a large ship on the ocean floor, and then they slipped into the cold water and descended, spreading out. Sidney insisted they all carry fish knives in scabbards, in case they had to cut through ropes or whatever.

They searched for almost an hour, coming up for fresh oxygen tanks, then going back down, as the sun sank lower in the sky. Finally old Anselmo signaled Sidney frantically, pointing down and to the south. Sidney swam over and, on the bottom, perhaps six fathoms, or forty feet, down – there it was! Brownish-gray, covered in mud and slime, was the clear outline of the wooden sailing ship with steam-powered sidewheels, the *Estrella del Sur*! And the search inside the ship began.

DRAWN FROM MEMORY
BY L. SID CAMP —
AFTER MY ADVENTURE

Fishing boat chartered by Sidney

CHAPTER 22

And they found it! Or rather Sidney found it. He figured
the solid silver mother and child – and pistol – would be
in the ship's safe, in the purser's cabin, and it was. As he
swam in, he saw that the door to the safe was open; no
doubt the purser had removed any cash as the ship was
going down, but the statue would have been far too heavy
to worry about. And there in the open safe, which was
an iron box perhaps three by five feet and three feet or
so deep, was a two-foot-high lump of something inside a
bulky canvas bag. With his knife he cut open the rotting
bag and stared at the tarnish-blackened *Virgen y Niño con
Pistola*!

Sidney swam back to where he knew a long rope
from the fishing boat was loosely tied to a railing of the

Estrella del Sur, untied it and swam with the end of the rope back to the purser's cabin. There he looped the rope under an arm of *la Virgen*, tied a tight knot, and gave it a series of tugs. After a few moments, someone up top began hoisting the reliquary upward.

Then, as Sidney guided the heavy piece through the purser's cabin door and out onto the tilted deck, he saw something that made his blood run cold. An eye, yellow and as big as a basketball, was looking at him from the far side of the sunken ship's rail. Then he saw the long body to which the eye belonged, a gray mass at least a dozen feet long, and a tangle of massive tentacles, equally long. One tentacle was wrapped around the ship's rail, and another was reaching out for Sidney. Although a professor of Medieval Spanish Literature and not biology, Sidney nevertheless recognized the monster as *Architeuthis Dux*, the giant squid whose habitat included the waters off the Iberian Peninsula.

As he stood in the purser's cabin doorway, paralyzed with fear, he saw in another of the great creature's writhing tentacles a struggling old Anselmo. At that moment, the giant squid's huge, parrot-like beak chomped down on Anselmo's torso; clouds of dark red blood billowed all about the old one. Sidney was horrified, and it spurred him into action.

Now, Sidney had seen enough movies in his life in which giant squids attacked the films' heroes while they were diving in the ocean. And these men had always fought off the beast, armed only with a knife. He recalled a few of the more memorable man-versus-giant squid encounters he had seen since he was a child: first, Tarzan – Johnny Weissmueller, then Lex Barker – followed by James Mason as Captain Nemo of the *Nautilus*, John Wayne, and even James Bond. And all of them had prevailed by thrusting their knives into one of the squid's huge eyes. So that, Sidney decided, is what he must do, if he were to have any hope of making the creature release poor old Anselmo. He propelled himself forward, toward the hideous great yellow eye, and he plunged his knife into it.

Appearance of the giant squid

CHAPTER 23

Back on the deck of Captain Juan's fishing boat, the crew was hovered around a dying Anselmo. The horrible giant squid had mercifully fled the scene after Sidney's knife attack, and Sidney had brought the old fellow up. The heavy reliquary had not created much of a stir when it was hauled up with the rope; tarnished as it was, it just looked like a statue made of lead, or clay. But Sidney knew that with some silver polish and "elbow grease", it would shine like the beautiful precious metal work of art it was. Now he had only to get it to the archbishop at the Cathedral of Santiago de Compostela, its original destination back in 1877. But his thoughts were interrupted by a cry from Pancho.

"*Señor!* A boat! Coming up fast! And I think it is those men who locked us in the castle tower!" He was watching an oncoming motorized fishing vessel through a brass spyglass. The boat was clearly more powerful than their own craft, as the wake being displaced was high and frothy, and boat itself was bouncing up and down vigorously, indicating high speed. They had obviously located and kept track of the escaped Sidney and Pancho, and they had to know that whatever the foreigner who called himself el Cid and his lackey were up to, it would be equally of interest to them. The boat of the Maluco men was closing; it would not be too long before they were alongside. Sidney, Pancho, Captain Juan and the fourth man, the mate, watched as the other boat drew nearer. It was now perhaps fifty meters away.

Suddenly a great tentacle looped over the bow of the Maluco men's boat, then another. The blinded giant squid had been in the path of the oncoming boat and, enraged, it was set to "take it out" on any boat, and the one it next encountered was that of the vessel of the Maluco men. Screams of fear could be heard from their boat, which had slowed considerably. Perhaps another tentacle had wrapped itself around the propeller. Sidney and his companions cheered with relief.

Captain Juan started up his fishing boat's small engine and they began chugging away from the area. In a couple of minutes las Rocas de Guano were well astern, as was the giant squid-enveloped boat of the Malucos Galegos men. The Good Guys were getting away!

DRAWN FROM MEMORY
BY L. SID CAMP —
AFTER MY ADVENTURE

The blinded squid attacks the Maluco men's boat

CHAPTER 24

En route back to the mainland in the setting sun, Sidney was marveling over the fabulous two-foot-high, silver statue of *Virgen el Niño con Pistola* when Captain Juan came up to him.

"*Señor* Cid," he said, "Anselmo, the *viejo* who was bitten by the squid, is dying, but he desires to speak with you before death takes him. He says it is important. Perhaps I should tell you: he has no family or loved ones. I hope you will see him."

Sidney immediately went the old one. A dying man's wish is not to be ignored, he told himself. He found the old fisherman in the stern of the boat, propped up somewhat on some sacks. He quickly ascertained that the old fellow would indeed die soon; the giant squid's powerful beak had cut his abdomen almost in two; his entrails were grotesquely hanging out. But the man was conscious.

"One did want to seeth me, fusty one?" Sidney asked gently.

"Aye," replied the mortally wounded man. "Although I am not religious, it will be a confession of sorts."

"So beest t," replied Sidney, waving the other man away.

"Sire," croaked *el viejo*, "I heard your friend Pancho say that you were el Cid Campeador reincarnate, and he told me all you had accomplished. Still, I scoffed at the thought. But now I see it is true. No one else could have done all you have. Thus it is to you and you alone I must divulge a truth I have held within my breast for lo these many decades."

"Speaketh, fusty one."

DRAWN FROM MEMORY
BY L. SID CAMP —
AFTER MY ADVENTURE

Old Anselmo

"*Señor* Cid, you must understand that I was brought up in a true communist family. My father, a young army officer for the republic, was a faithful Party member most of his life. And through his loyalty to the Party and his many years of toil toward the goal of the workers' paradise, he was chosen to assist in the transfer of all the gold reserves of the republic from Madrid to the Soviet Union in October 1936. Surely you know of what I speak?"

"Aye," said Sidney, nodding. He remembered reading that Juan Negrín, the republic's Minister of Finance under President and Council of Ministers head Francisco Largo Caballero, "the Spanish Lenin", had ordered all of the nation's gold supply – said to have been one of the largest in the world – shipped to the Soviet Union "for safekeeping" and to purchase war materiel. It was also recorded that Joseph Stalin, upon hearing about the plan, laughed and commented. "The Spanish will never see their gold again, as they do not see their ears now!" The gold, it was estimated, was of sufficient quantity to completely pave over the vast Red Square in Moscow. Some 460 tons of gold were involved, at current rates the value of some twenty billion dollars.

"Then you know," the old man went on, "that the plan was to transfer the gold by truck convoy from a Madrid expected to fall to Franco's forces at any time, to

Cartagena on the coast, for shipment by sea to Odessa." The man paused to cough up blood.

"Aye, mine own cousin, wend on," said Sidney. He wished there were something, anything, he could do for the poor creature.

"The plan," the old one continued, "was of course absolutely top secret. Only a very few men, including Comrade Stalin, knew of the venture. The highway from Madrid to Cartagena was closed to all traffic during the move. And all crossroads and side roads were blocked off for many hours. The convoy of trucks left Madrid in the dark of night – but it never reached Cartagena. It simply disappeared from the face of the earth. Naturally, a massive search was instigated, but to no avail. The convoy and all the men – except my father – were gone. Finally, after much waiting at the port in Cartagena, the ship meant to carry the gold sailed without it. Only my father knew what had happened to it."

"And yond wast . . .?" asked Sidney.

The dying fisherman coughed and went on. "My father, a young *teniente* and Party member, had been assigned to the last vehicle in the convoy, meant to watch for any persons leaving one of the trucks en route, who might tell others about the gold. He had a driver, a private, but that soldier, also a Party member, was struck with dysentery just before departure from Madrid and had to drop out. Thus my father alone drove the car, a Renault liberated earlier from a fascist fatcat, at the end of convoy. Incidentally, that sick driver, the private, died mysteriously a few hours later.

"Thirty-one kilometers northwest of Cartagena there is a line of barren cliffs into which mines for lead had been dug in the previous century. A small line of rail racks for the ore carts still ran from just outside the entrance and on into the mine. But the mine had not been used in many years.

"Anyway, as the convoy was approaching this area in the very early morning, an Italian fighter-bomber, a Breda Ba.65 based on Mallorca, spotted the line of trucks and made a clumsy attempt to strafe them, but all the trucks survived the first pass. The officer in charge of the convoy saw the old mine entrance not far from the highway and had his driver immediately swing his truck off it and onto a rough wagon track leading to the mine entrance. All the trucks followed. In the meantime, the Italian plane was circling around for another pass.

October 1936: Gold caravan leaves Madrid

"The last truck was just entering the mine entrance when the fighter-bomber dove for the opening, no doubt trying to emulate the German Stuka dive bombers he had seen in action, to blow up the entrance and thus sealing up the trucks and men – forever. He of course had no idea what was in those trucks.

"My father's car was the only vehicle in the convoy which did not make it into the mine. It seemed that when he turned off the highway and onto the wagon track, his car broke an axle. And now the Italian plane was making its dive toward the mine entrance. But as I say, the pilot was Italian, not German, and he failed to pull out of his dive in time. His plane crashed into the mine entrance and all his bombs and fuel exploded, causing an avalanche which completely sealed the gold convoy within the cliff face. And it is still there."

Sidney mused. "A fascinating story. But wherefore bid me all this? Especially now . . ." he gestured hopelessly at the man's ruined abdomen. Surely this old fellow couldn't last much longer.

"Because I – and only I – know exactly where that buried mine and its treasure convoy are located!" He tried to smile triumphantly, but it came out as more of a grimace. "You see, my father never told a soul about all this – except me, some years ago."

"But wherefore?" queried Sidney. "Didst that gent not wanteth the republic to beest able to salvage the gold? Or at least tryeth?"

"*No, señor,*" was the reply. "Because before the convoy left Madrid with the gold, he was told that if he said anything about the gold to anyone, they – the Party – would execute his wife, my mother. After the incident at the mine, he walked for many kilometers to a store with a telephone, where he called a neighbor of my mother in Madrid – we had no phone, you see – to tell my mother he was all right. He was advised by the neighbor that the night he left for Cartagena, some men wearing black leather overcoats came to our home – Party men, because they came in a car with a red star on the door . . . and took my mother away. Her body was found the next morning, in the Retiro Park. Thus my father realized that the Party had taken no chances of him telling his wife about the gold. He realized then that if the gold had been delivered, he, too, would have been killed. He subsequently fled to France, returning only after Franco's death. And while my father was a communist, I was never a Party member.

"And that," bespoke the horribly injured man, now whispering, "is why he turned against the Party and told no one. But the gold is there yet. Exactly thirty-one kilometers northwestward along the old Madrid-Cartagena highway, there is an old wagon track leading toward some distant barren cliffs to the east. At their base, some old ore cart rail tracks disappear into mounds of earth and rock. Behind that is the old lead mine – and the gold convoy."

"And Stalin?" asked Sidney.

"He was going to deny having received the gold anyway. Now he would just be telling the truth. Although I think the republican leaders believed that he had somehow actually gotten it. But in fact, he had no idea as to what happened to it.

Sidney was dumbstruck. Twenty billion dollars in gold, thirty-one kilometers northwest of Cartagena! What a destitute Spain could do with that today! He looked back at the old man and started to ask another question, but the poor fellow was dead.

CHAPTER 25

The old archbishop was, as they say, pleased as punch.
Nay, more pleased than that. More like pleased as Ponche
Caballero, a "gentleman's punch" liqueur. He was on his
knees in his private office of the Cathedral of Santiago
de Compostela, crossing himself over and over, a beatific
expression on his face. In front of him, on a table, was
la Virgen y Niño con Pistola, gleaming as though brand
new. A shaft of sunlight coming through a high window
spotlighted the holy reliquary dramatically.

Sidney had taken the heavy Madonna and child (and
pistol) to his room in the Hotel de los Reyes Católicos
and had sent Pancho out to buy some silver polish. Then,
using towels from the bathroom, the two men had cleaned
and polished the statue set until it shone like silver fire.

He telephoned the archbishop's office, but word of the miraculous discovery had already reached the old prelate. Guarded by a phalanx of city policemen, *la Virgen y Niño con Pistola* was then trundled across the wide plaza separating the hotel and the cathedral and presented to a speechless archbishop.

His Eminence, thrilled beyond words to have this magnificent holy object finally at rest where it belonged, after so many years on the ocean bottom, had telephoned both the king and the prime minister in Madrid with the good news; Both men and their entourages promised to be in Santiago – along with the media, of course – the following day. What a joyous occasion it would be for Spain!

The news on the television that night and the newspapers the next morning were of course saturated with the story. Sidney's picture, and that of Pancho as well, were everywhere, and all of "el Cid's" many accomplishments were enumerated, over and over. The coming of the king and the prime minister simply underlined the importance of the great event. Sidney and Pancho met with both officials, separately, receiving their thanks and promises to help in any way possible. The queen accompanied her husband and was delightful, while the prime minister was surrounded by ministers and "yes-men", as Sidney mentally categorized them.

DRAWN FROM MEMORY
BY L. SID CAMP —
AFTER MY ADVENTURE

The Cathedral of Santiago de Compostela

It was during these meetings that Sidney broached the story of the lost Spanish gold of 1936, all twenty billion dollars' worth, privately to the king and the prime minister. Needless to say, both men were incredulous, although "el Cid's" many successes lent serious credence to what would otherwise no doubt have been dismissed as a pipe dream. At Sidney's request, both men promised to tell no one until the time came, but, being a politician, the prime minister lied and told his aides. Some of the PM's retinue then tried to press Sidney for the details as to the location of the trove, but the professor was firm here; no, he would personally lead them to the place in due course, but first he wanted to visit the Alahambra in Granada, another place he had missed in 1960. Some of the men with the prime minister became rather heated in trying to press their point, but the prime minister himself followed the king's lead here and "backed off." All in due course, it was agreed.

CHAPTER 26

With the virtual army of reporters in Santiago, Sidney and Pancho found it expedient to depart the city at three o'clock in the morning, lest they be followed by a caravan of media vans and cars. Sidney left notes for the king and prime minister. They stayed off the *autopistas*, as they knew the media people would be monitoring those super highways. They took two days to make the five hundred mile trip, overnighting en route in Talavera de la Reina.

The king had told Sidney that as a gesture of appreciation for his salvaging *la Virgen y Niño con Pistola*, he would have him and Pancho met upon arrival at the Alhambra by a retinue of some twenty *aides de camp*, who would see to their every need and would even provide special guest rooms for them right there in the

Alhambra itself. In addition, realizing that Sidney had spent considerable sums of his own money to pay all costs involved in the recovery of the silver reliquary, the king ordered an aide to present Sidney with a fat envelope; when the professor opened it later, he found that it contained a small fortune in euros. And now he and Pancho were to be met at the Alhambra by twenty of the king's staff. It was all mind-boggling.

As they drove into the outskirts of Granada, Sidney saw a shop with a sign across the front: *Museo del Jamón.* In the big plate glass window hung an array of hams, the famous *jamón de jabugo,* Spain's world-renowned, air cured ham from pigs fed on acorns – the best ham in the world, according to many experts. The place was of course a store, not a museum, but such *tiendas* were routinely called *museos del jamón.* Sidney pulled the jeep up to the front door and turned off the ignition.

"Pancho, in the Unit'd States, at which hour one calleth on cater-cousins f'r dinn'r, tis customary to bringeth a gift such as floweth'rs 'r a bombard of wine as a gift. Well, we art did suppose to beest hath met by twenty p'rsons of the king's staff at the Alhambra and I bethink it only prop'r yond we cometh bearing gifts. We art not Greeks, aft'r all."

"No, *señor*," replied Pancho. "I am Spanish, and you are American!"

"Quite correct Pancho! Cometh!" he entered the store, Pancho following. At the counter he addressed a white-coated clerk.

"Twenty-two of your finest *jamónes de jabugo*, my friend!" he cried.

"Twenty-two!" Pancho blurted.

"Yes, Pancho, twenty for our hosts, and one each for thee and me!"

"But, sire, that will cost a fortune! These hams are very expensive!"

"And I am very rich, grant you mercy to the king!" Sidney flourished the fat envelope full of euros.

Sidney asked the clerk if, under the circumstances, the other twenty hams could be delivered to the Alhambra. When the dazed man finally regained his senses, he replied that, *si*, it could be done. The store had three men and a large van and he could hire seventeen more boys and men and dress them in white coats, to do the job, although it would be expensive.

DRAWN FROM MEMORY
BY L. SID CAMP —
AFTER MY ADVENTURE

Jamón de jabugo

Sidney was delighted, and he counted out the required stack of euros on the counter top. Then he and Pancho waited patiently as the clerk made a series of telephone calls, rounding up the other deliverymen, then wrapping all the big hams in white butcher's paper. After half an hour or so, all were there, and a caravan comprised of Sidney's Jeep, the van with the hams and ten men and boys, and two cars with a total of ten more men and boys set out for the Alahambra. All wore white, doctor-like coats – even Sidney and Pancho, "Just to joineth the excitement! We shall behold liketh a white army arm'd with hams!"

CHAPTER 27

What Sidney and Pancho – and the deliverymen – did not know was that at that very moment the venerable old Alhambra was under siege, by yet another of those groups of crazed muslims who would like to destroy everything and everybody, often including themselves. Led by a wild-eyed, bearded man called Ali bin Belchin, some fifteen self-styled Sons of Allah had stormed the Alhambra and taken prisoner not only the historic complex's staff, but also the twenty dignataries sent by the king and several tourists. Wielding a terrifying array of curved, medieval scimitars, they held their captives huddled together in the famed Court of the Lions, an open courtyard enclosed by magnificent filigreed columns and, in the center, a lovely fountain surrounded by stone lions – which gave the place its name.

"What is your purpose?" asked the curator of the great museum, of the leader, bin Belchin. Without hesitation, the bearded one replied.

"We will destroy this abominable structure! Raze it to the ground! And all you infidels with it!"

"But why?" pleaded the curator, an old gentleman of advanced years. "Surely you know that the Alhambra was constructed five to eight hundred years ago by muslims like yourselves! Why would you want to destroy it?"

"Hah!" retorted bin Belchin. "Muslims, yes. But not like ourselves. The Alhambra was built by muslims of the Nasrid Dynasty, of the Emirate of Granada! Wrong sect, you see. Why, if your Protestants built such a place, would not the Catholics want to destroy it?"

The curator sputtered, "Why, no, of course not! We . . ."

But the terrorist chief shouted him down. "Of course you would! Just as ISIS has destroyed the muslim mosques of Nimrud and Nineveh in Iraq! And the muslims of Asar-Dine have obliterated the so-called muslim treasures of

Timbuctu! We didn't build it, so we must destroy it! We, the Sons of Allah – actually, our full name is the Sons and Second Cousins of Allah, but that is too long for newspaper headlines – anyway, we have the explosives and we will level this abomination and all infidels within it!" The old curator noticed for the first time that the fifteen terrorists all wore bomb vests.

Now, it was at this moment that Sidney and his *jamón* caravan drove up to the Alhambra's front entrance, on the mountaintop high above the city of Granada. He thought it strange that he was able to do so in such easy fashion and that there were no guards or even ticket sellers or collectors in evidence. And no tourists. Well, so much the better. He instructed the twenty white-coated deliverymen to each take one ham – they were heavy things, wrapped in the white butcher's paper and weighing probably forty pounds apiece – and hold it in front, clutching the precious meat to their chests as they would an infant. They were to march in, single file, with himself in the lead and Pancho second. Sidney and Pancho, too, would be bearing their own hams, just in case they needed an extra or two. They set off to find their greeting party from the king, a white-coated column of twenty-two men and boys, each bearing a precious, heavy gift of *jamón de jabugo*.

DRAWN FROM MEMORY
BY L. SID CAMP ——
AFTER MY ADVENTURE

Court of the Lions

They walked from hall to hall, seeing nobody. This is strange, Sidney told himself. Where are the tourists? Where are the usual museum guards? At last they passed a sign pointing the way to the celebrated Court of the Lions, probably the most-photographed part of the Alhambra. As they entered the open-air patio, they saw a frightened-looking mass of people huddled against a far wall, probably some fifty or more of them, several of them in the white *jellaba* of the arab wearing traditional dress, and the others in Western attire. Sidney, the first of his lot to enter, stopped and smiled. The deliverymen followed and lined the wall behind him.

"I bringeth thee greetings from the king." he cried, smiling.

But the group across the way did not seemed pleased. Oddly, the ones in the back seemed to show fear, while those in front, wearing white flowing robes with what looked like gray life jackets, all looked angry. One of the latter lot stepped forward.

"What is this?" demanded bin Belchin. "What are you? Police? Army bomb squad? And since when has a unit such as yours worn white uniforms? We are not in the snows of Russia, you fools! And you very cleverly cover your weapons with white paper – so as not to alarm the idiot Spanish masses, I presume. Well, it will do you no good here! One shot into any one of our sacred group of the Sons of Allah will cause his bomb vest to explode. And that, in turn, will detonate all our other bomb vests! The precious Alhambra – and you – will all be destroyed!"

"And thee, as well," replied Sidney. He had put his ham under his white coat. Buttoned up, the coat helped to support the heavy ham. It made Sidney look very fat.

"Yes, including us," sneered the terrorist leader. "But, unlike you, we will immediately ascend to Paradise, where 72 virgins will be awaiting each of my men!"

"Thy men?" asked Sidney. What about thee? No virgins f'r thee?"

"Ha!" was the scornful reply. "You stupid infidel! You see, as a prophet myself, I am eligible to speak directly with the prophet Mohammed, who in turn speaks directly with Allah! And last night we, uh, made a deal. The prophet himself promised me that if I carried out this mission successfully, then I personally would be rewarded not with the ususal 72 virgins, but with 144! A full gross! And all with big, well, you know. So none of us are afraid to die! Of course, should I manage to survive, I would carry on our sacred work! It is too bad for you that you and your infidel companions have nothing like our Paradise to look forward to!"

Sidney stepped closer, and bin Belchin withdrew his huge, shiny scimitar from the scabbard hanging from the green sash around the waist of his white *jellaba*, just below his bomb vest.

"P'rhaps thee hast heard of me, of late," said Sidney, his hands on his stomach, helping to hold up the big ham under his white coat. "I am the one being ref'rr'd to as el Cid Campeador."

The lead muslim blinked, then apparently a little less sure of himself, said, "Ha! Returned from the dead, are you? After all these centuries? Well, praise be to Allah, we shall see just how immortal you really are!" And with that, he hurled his thirty-inch-long scimitar, end over end, at Sidney's chest. A loud gasp poured out from all the non-muslims in the Court of Lions. The muslims grinned fiercely.

CHAPTER 28

The gleaming blade of the lethal weapon penetrated Sidney's white coat and the ham beneath it with a loud *thoonk*, by a good three or four inches. A woman among the captives screamed; men gasped.

Sidney thought to himself, you bugger! You have spoilt my beautiful *jamón de jabugo!* Then, leaving the wicked blade in place, he advanced several steps closer to bin Belchin, whose eyes were now standing out as though on stems.

"Begone, thee mere mortals!" cried Sidney, mustering up more apparent courage than he actually felt. Then he turned to the line of white-coated deliverymen standing – in horror, it is true – against a wall behind him and shouted,

"Drop of sorrow from paper from thy packages, men! Alloweth those folk seeth our true armaments!" Pancho translated, and, after a moment's hesitation, the line of men began ripping the white butcher's paper off the big hams.

"Anon, hold those folk up and out, and advance!" And the deliverymen did so.

Now the terrorists could see what it was that the men held and with which they were moving ever closer. Dark and evil eyes bulged at the sight.

"The flesh one dare not speak its name!" one of the Sons of Allah shouted out, and all his companions began backing up, looks of horror on their visages.

Sidney, the ugly scimitar still protruding from his chest, turned to the advancing phalanx of ham bearers and bawled, "Keepeth advancing, men! Advance until thy *jamones* art pressing against these evil-doers!" And the deliverymen did keep advancing, if hesitatingly, as they seemed to understand the situation and what it was that Sidney was attempting to accomplish. The terrorists, on the other hand, were clearly in retreat. Having seen their leader's scimitar having no affect after apparently penetrating the breast of the man they all now assumed was indeed the reincarnated Cid, they made no attempt to draw their own blades. Rather, their minds were all on escape. The 72 virgins could wait.

Sidney pointed to the doorway through which he and the deliverymen had recently entered and shouted, "Through yond doth'r and out on the street thy shall findeth a white van big enow to accommodate all of thee! Wend to't, and begone! Or else these *jamones* shall beest did press 'gainst each one of thee, and thee shall beest condemned to the fires of Fibbertigibbet! Yond is hell to thee! Nay virgins f'r thee – just an ev'rlasting roasting in the fires! Chooseth! Yond fate – 'r escapeth! Go! Apace!"

And every one of the Sons and Second Cousins of Allah ran for the doorway and on through the other halls and rooms of the Alhambra, to the street outside. There they found the large white van, with the key in the ignition. They all piled in hurridly, bin Belchin at the wheel and one other riding "shotgun." The other thirteen piled into the back. With tires squealing, the van pulled out and into the street and headed down the mountain on which the Alhambra was situated, toward the city of Granada.

Now, with thirteen men, all of them wearing bomb vests activated by the wearer pulling on a little cord on the front of the vest, like the chain to a table lamp, and all of them tightly packed, standing, in the back of the van, with the van bouncing and swerving around the winding mountain road, it was virtually inevitable that in the grabbing and struggling to remain erect, someone would inadvertently brush down against or otherwise yank one of the bomb cords. As the big white van hurtled around a sharp mountain road curve, it suddenly exploded in a monumental loud flash and ball of fire and, immediately following, a billowing cloud of smoke that lingered over the mountainside for a long time. The van was blown into a million pieces, as were the Sons and Second Cousins of Allah. It was just fortunate that no cars were near when the great cataclysm occurred.

The Sons of Allah en route to their reward

CHAPTER 29

Back in the Alahambra, Sidney and the others heard the explosion, and all knew what it meant. They were truly safe now. Sidney and Pancho removed their white butchers' coats and the king's representatives, led by a distinguished-looking older man with white hair and wearing a red-and-yellow royal sash diagonally across his chest and his smart, white, military-style attire, and identifying himself as Don Fulano, the Duque de Nuque, confidante to the king, congratulated Sidney – and, secondarily, Pancho – for delivering them from the clutches of the evil Ali bin Belchin. The duke presented Sidney with a handsome ribboned medal and hinted that, in light of the day's happenings, there would undoubtedly be others to come. Sidney thanked the gentlemen profusely and reciprocated by presenting them with the *jamónes de jabugo*, which they were quite obviously delighted to receive. Sidney tipped the deliverymen and thanked them for their help. They all hurried off to tell others what had happened.

The Duque de Nuque then formally invited Sidney – and Pancho – to meet with the king in Madrid, at the Royal Palace. Sidney told him that he had met with the king quite recently in Santiago de Compostela, but the royal emissary then explained that something new had come up, and "el Nuevo Cid" was needed immediately. What on earth could this be about, Sidney wondered.

Sidney explained that he still had the Alhambra to see, and the duke and his entourage all made deprecating sounds, assuring him that of course that could be arranged, *right now*. The duke snapped his fingers and the head curator of the Alhambra appeared at his side like a rabbit out of a hat, whereupon he assured the duke that a personal guided tour of the Alhambra would be provided to Sidney – and Pancho – forthwith. The duke said "Excellent!" and clapped his hands twice. A uniformed airline pilot appeared, and the duke gave him instructions to go immediately to the local airport and have the king's private jet readied for takeoff in one hour. The pilot saluted and hurried from the room.

The Duque de Nuque

Sidney and Pancho then received their promised personal tour of the Alhambra, guided by the head curator himself. Sidney was overwhelmed – and Pancho liked it too. And just to think: without them, this beauty would be all gone.

After the tour, the two were shown to their private guest rooms there in the Alhambra to freshen up, prior to their departure for the airport. Sidney had been assured that someone would drive Babieca the Jeep to Madrid, and he had thus relinquished the keys.

Sidney walked out onto the ground floor patio fronting his room, and he beheld a breathtaking view of the Generalife, part of the great Alhambra complex. Slender cypress trees and stately palms towered over manicured gardens, while Moorish fountains bubbled and splashed. It was beautiful!

But suddenly the serenity was disturbed. A black-bearded man wearing a stained green teeshirt emblazoned with the words *Partido de Soñadores Andalucistas* in white pushed his way through the big hedge which gave the patio privacy. And the man was pointing a pistol at Sidney.

"So!" he hissed. "You are the one who calls himself el Cid! You, who would make Spain whole again!

With everybody kowtowing to a king and government in Madrid! Well, we of the PSA – the Soñadores Andalucistas – are here to stop you! Soon the green and white flag of Andalucia will be the *only* flag flying over our own independent country! You have met your – eh?" The bearded one looked back over his shoulder, toward the hedge. Someone else was there, calling out to him in a stage whisper.

"Paco!" the voice called out.

"Qué?" replied the man with the gun. "What do you want? I am telling this fool 'el Cid' that he . . ."

"Paco! It is important!" the other voice called out hoarsely.

"O, por Diós!" sighed the gunman, then backing up to the hedge. "All right! Now, what is it?" The hidden man replied in that same stage whisper that Sidney could hear.

"Paco!" came the voice from the hedge. "I have only this moment learned that just today, this afternoon, this man, er, el Cid, was stabbed through the heart by a Moorish scimitar and yet did not die! In turn, he personally destroyed all the Sons of Allah and their leader, Ali bin Belchin! They are no more! Paco! I think this is the real Cid!"

DRAWN FROM MEMORY
BY L. SID CAMP —
AFTER MY ADVENTURE

The Alhambra

"Mierda!" cursed the man called Paco, pausing to scratch his beard with the end of his gunbarrel. Then he turned back to face Sidney. Now he was smiling. Although the smile quivered a bit.

"Señor! I, ah, um, I was just making a joke, you understand? Er, ha, ha. *Sí,* a joke! Well, I must go now!" And he lurched back into the hedge and was gone.

CHAPTER 30

Sidney and Pancho were agog – again. This time at the beauty and opulence of the Royal Palace in Madrid. It was everything a royal palace should be, and more. From a small airport just outside Madrid, not the busy international one at Barajas, they had been driven in a black limo to an undistinguished back entrance to the palace. The front of the palace, the Duque de Nuque explained, was jammed with protesters demanding – what? Something. Something to be done about Spain's precarious condition. Unemployment was at an all-time high, prices were soaring, every province seemed to be demanding independence, the people were not happy. Down at the Cortés, the parliament building, it was the same. The masses were demanding – something, anything, everything.

Sidney and Pancho were shown into an elaborate sitting room and asked to seat themselves on what Sidney thought to be Louis XV chairs. A huge portrait of a haughty Charles the Third on horseback graced the far wall. After a few minutes, the king entered, followed by the prime minister. Both greeted Sidney effusively. They also said hello to Pancho. The king turned things over to the PM, who bowed to His Majesty and then spoke directly to Sidney.

"*Señor* Camp. Spain is grateful for all you have done for this nation (Sidney ducked his head in acknowledgement). We just have one more thing to ask of you – in addition, of course, to the most urgent matter of the Spanish gold, because this matter cannot wait.

"You see," went on the PM, "we are currently besieged not only by the throngs of Spanish demonstrators demanding that we, the government, and even the king, do something – something, anything, that will make things better, put people back to work, reduce prices, as I say, anything. But in the meantime, unknown to the average 'man on the street', we are faced with an even bigger problem, and one which takes precedence for the moment over locating the lost Spanish gold.

"Only today we received a communication from Brussels – that is, the seat of the European Union – that a delegation of highly placed bureaucrats led by one Mijneer Adolf Rode van Plakband is descending upon us, to demand we know not yet what, but we suspect and fear it may be a directive to 'pay or get out'. Out of the EU, that is. And that would be disastrous for us. Now, we know of your information about the lost gold and, believe me, that could be a lifesaver for us. But, even in the best of circumstances, the finding and recovery of it would undoubtedly require much time and effort. Yet these men from Brussels (here the prime minister paused to shake his head and make a noise like *phtt!*) will want *immediate* satisfaction! Now, we know that this request is *most* unusual, but we desperately need help. And you, who have in recent days done *so much* to help Spain, we turn to in our hour of need. Oh, please, *Señor* Camp – *Señor* el Cid – please help us! What are we to do?" The PM dropped his head; his plea was finished.

DRAWN FROM MEMORY
BY L. SID CAMP —
AFTER MY ADVENTURE

The EU Delegation from Brussels

CHAPTER 31

Sidney thought for a moment. "Art all these men from Brussels?" he asked. The answer was positive. "And how longeth shall those gents beest h're?" Well, nobody knew; until the problem – whatever it was – was resolved, one presumed.

Sidney thought – and thought. Finally he said, "Thee wanteth timeth, right?" The king and the prime minister nodded their heads vigorously.

"Well, then," said "the new" Cid, "issue an ord'r, effective immediately, yond *nay restaurants*, enwheeling hotels, shall serve *pomme frites* 'r waffles."

"What?" said both the king and the PM, openmouthed.

"Yond is what those gents consume," explained Sidney. "Without 't, those gents are liketh a dog with an exsufflicate bowl! Charge all thy kitchens in the Madrid area to immediately cease serving *pomme frites* and waffles!"

The order was strange, but it was quickly transmitted to every Madrid area establishment serving food. The penalty for disregarding the order was draconian, so all establishments complied. It was not long before the first complaints began to come in – from the Brussels delegation. Room service in the hotel where the delegation was staying reported that they had multiple and repeated orders for *pommes frites*, which they could not fill. The next morning, there were no waffles available. An uproar among the VIPs from Brussels was reported. Indeed, it developed into a near riot: the men of the delegation demanded *pommes frites* and waffles. Yet there were none to be had. Back to Brussels! they demanded. And back to Brussels they went. "You will hear from us!" cried one of the men, a Monsieur Pierre Papier-Poussoir, as he and his retinue left. And that was fine with their Spanish counterparts. It gave them what they needed so badly: time!

DRAWN FROM MEMORY
BY L. SID CAMP —
AFTER MY ADVENTURE

Belgian food

After the Belgians' departure, it was learned that they had, in their frustration over no *pommes frites* or waffles, planned to stage a food fight in their hotel dining room, but the required paperwork for such an event would require simply too much time and so they left without having committed to the act.

CHAPTER 32

Now it was time to go get the famed Lost Gold! It took three days to arrange but at last a full battalion, five hundred men, of the Spanish military's finest, the legendary Spanish Legion – formerly the Spanish Foreign Legion, but today an all-Spaniard outfit – better known as the Tercio, was ready to go. With them were their own engineers, with earth-moving equipment and dynamite. And orders had gone out to scour the military bases of the nation for heavy duty trucks capable of hauling 460 tons of heavy metal. That would mean at least one hundred such vehicles, which would be needed if the gold was found in its entirety. Once the "strike" was made, the trucks would be directed to the Cartagena area from all over the country. In the meantime, the Spanish Legion forces would guard the site. The media, of course, had not been alerted, although how long the project could remain a secret was anybody's guess.

As it was, the military convoy leaving from Madrid before dawn was an impressive one: twenty-five canvas-covered trucks carrying twenty men each, four flatbed tractor-trailers hauling the heavy earth-moving equipment, several staff cars for the officers, and limos for the politicians and the king's representatives, and Sidney and Pancho in Bibieca, in the lead – except for the four motorcycle military policemen forging a path out front, their sirens blaring. With the heavy trucks, it was slow going, and the 215 mile trip took them some eight hours or so.

It was early afternoon when they reached the area described by old Anselmo. Earlier, the government people had researched all information pertaining to old lead mines of the late nineteenth century in this area, and three possibles had been found in the records. Two were approximately thirty-one kilometers northwest of Cartagena, while the third was one and a half kilometers still further north. Teams of military engineers were sent out to search for all three sites, looking especially for a blocked mine entrance with a small ore cart rail track leading to it. The crashed Italian fighter-bomber, or rather any remains of it, would most probably have been plundered by junk hunters in the intervening years.

The search began about one p.m., and some two hours later the colonel in charge of the engineers received a call on his cell phone, with the report that the searchers believed they had found the old mine entrance, buried under tons of rubble. The big earth-moving machines were immediately dispatched to the site in question, and work was begun without delay. Sidney was told of the probable find, and he and Pancho rode in Babieca to the place, following a Legion Jeep carrying the commanding officer. Another Jeep brought three of the top civilian VIPs. The limos could not negotiate the rough terrain.

Once they got up close, they all could see many small remnants of the Italian fighter-bomber which had not been salvaged for junk over the years by the locals: a strip of badly bent metal and a few twisted bolts here, pieces of shattered plexiglass and burned pieces of rubber there, but nothing substantial.

DRAWN FROM MEMORY
BY L. SID CAMP —
AFTER MY ADVENTURE

Blocked entrance to the old lead mine

Some work was done, but the sun was setting, and so the military commander ordered it halted and the men assigned to pup tents which had been set up in the meantime. The VIPs, including Sidney and Pancho, got bigger tents, with battery-powered electric lights. The VIPs also got "Jiffy Johnnies", while the rank and file used latrines. A guard detachment was posted all around the site. Indeed, the guards had to "shoo off" a few curious locals who wanted to see What was going on. Mercifully, the area was mostly barren and desolate, hence few people living nearby.

CHAPTER 33

At first light, work was resumed. And another two hours or so later, a cheer went up when the open shaft of the mine was finally uncovered. Anxious legionnaires were held back from the entrance by officers, while Sidney and Pancho, accompanied by the commander and several government and royal personages cautiously entered the yawning opening with powerful flashlights. And they did not have to go far before finding something. But it was not gold they encountered at this point. It was a pile of rag-covered skeletons, what was left of the men of the original convoy, all clustered around the blocked entranceway to the old mine. Pancho and several others crossed themselves furiously. All were stunned into silence.

The advance party tiptoed as best they could around

the human remains, which would of course have to be given proper burials in due course. They did not have to go far, for just ahead in the tunnel the flashlight beams picked out the rear end of a dusty olive-green truck. Its canvas cover over the rear portion sagged in rotten tatters, and the tires were all flat.

Pancho clambered up into the rear of the truck and shined his bright light over its contents, which were comprised of wooden crates stacked double, filling the cargo area. Someone handed him a crowbar and he prised a plank from the top of the uppermost crate. He peered inside, using his flashlight. Then he let out a big sigh of disappointment.

"What is 't, Pancho?" asked Sidney urgently.

"I think we have been played a joke on, *señor*."

"What doth thee cullonly?"

"It appears merely to be bars of lead, *señor*."

"Pancho!" said Sidney with great urgency. "Taketh the claw end of thy crowbar and scratch one of the bars!" Pancho did so, then shone his light on his work.

"*Señor el Cid! It is gold!* The tarnish merely made it *look* like lead!"

A babble of excitement from the search party filled the tunnel. Then a shout came from someone who had ventured further into the old mine. "The other trucks!" the man called out. "They are all here! We have found the gold convoy of 1936!"

DRAWN FROM MEMORY
BY L. SID CAMP —
AFTER MY ADVENTURE

But a tiny part of the Spanish gold trove

CHAPTER 34

Sidney had come prepared. He had felt – he had *known* – that they would find the gold, and he wanted to personally present the king with a bar of the precious metal. Thus back in Madrid he had sewn a stout canvas patch big enough to hold a standard brick, with a strong strap to go around his neck. After all, if he put a gold bar in his pants pocket, his trousers would fall down! He would clean the bar up later, just as he had done with *la Virgen y Niño con Pistola*. Pancho gave him a gray-coated bar and he slipped it into its special sack, then looped the strap around his neck. It was heavy, but he could manage it.

Just then there was a shout from the mine entrance, a soldier calling urgently for the *coronel*, his commander. The colonel ran to the daylight and listened to the man, then he hurried back to the group of dignitaries gathered around the last truck in the mine.

"Señores!" he called out. "We are being attacked! My man tells me some one thousand guerilla fighters of unknown origin are firing on my men! They are closing in on the mine entrance!"

Oh, no, thought Sid. It had just been too good to be true. With a discovery of this import, it was inevitable that someone would leak the information to *somebody*. He had a hunch who was involved, but he remained silent on this score. At that moment, a camouflage-clothed legionnaire who had earlier been pointed out to him as the Tercio's main intelligence officer appeared on the scene. In the background could be heard sporadic firing.

"Mi coronel!" the officer shouted to the *commandante*. "I know who the attackers are! They are a mixed bunch: Men of the ETX – the Basque independence people; the No Dretans – the Far Left of Cataluña; the CDC – the Chalados of Cantabria; the Malucos Galegos of Galicia; the Sons of the Sons of Allah; the SA – the Soñadores Andalucistas, and, worst of all, the Anarchists – and the Communist Party! The latter two are of course fighting for control, but what is important to us now is the fact that all are – at least temporarily – united in an effort to steal the gold! There must be a thousand of them! All

armed! Look! In the distance you can see the flags of the Anarchists and the Reds!" And sure enough, there they were, waving in the breeze.

Sidney was dismayed. Well, he supposed that it had been too much to hope that word would not somehow get out. But did this mean everything for which he had so diligently striven was all down the drain?

"This shalt not standeth!" he cried. "I shall parlay with those folk!" And procuring a white teeshirt from a legionnaire, which he affixed to a pole, he strode out to where the invaders were approaching.

DRAWN FROM MEMORY
BY L. SID CAMP —
AFTER MY ADVENTURE

Anarchist and Communist flags

CHAPTER 35

As Sidney, white flag in hand, drew nearer to the mixed mob, he could see that the intelligence officer's estimate of a thousand armed men was just about right. That meant the legionnaires were outnumbered two to one. And in the very front, walking toward him, were the eight leaders of the various groups. A step ahead of the rest were the Anarchist and Communist bosses. Sidney knew who they were from his experience in Barcelona. The fierce Anarchist woman whose name was Satana Iglesia Quemada, wore a sweatshirt with the circled letter A, as before, while the Communist, Camarada Titianio, wore his black leather coat and black peaked cap with a red star on it. When Sidney was upon them, everyone stopped. The Anarchist leader spoke first.

"We know who you are!" she cried, pointing at Sidney. "You are the *yanqui* who is going around Spain telling everyone that he is el Cid reincarnated, and that he cannot die! Well, we shall see about that!" And with that said, she pulled a long, wicked-looking Mauser pistol from a pocket of her baggy pants and shot Sidney right in the heart. The professor of Medieval Spanish Literature was blown backward and fell to earth on his back with a *thump!* The leaders of the mob and the men behind them all cheered heartily.

DRAWN FROM MEMORY
BY L. SUS CAMP —
AFTER MY ADVENTURE

She shot Sidney right in the heart

CHAPTER 36

Pancho, who had been watching Sidney and the enemy leaders from close by, behind a bush, was horrified to see his *señor* apparently shot dead. Without giving thought to his own safety, he bolted out from behind the bush and ran straight to his fallen hero. Pancho was lucky not to be shot himself, but the eight leaders merely laughed and made abusive remarks as he dragged his master back to the Legion's lines, leaving the white flag of truce lying on the ground.

Temporarily safe now, surrounded by legionnaires, Pancho frantically checked over Sidney. To his relief, he was alive! The gold bar hanging from his neck had stopped the bullet – just as the *jamón de jabugo* had stopped Ali bin Belchin's scimitar. But the professor had been knocked unconscious by the blow to his chest from the bullet.

Pancho looked about him. The legionnaires were readying their weapons, but they faced a force twice their number, which was now starting to creep toward the legionnaires formed up around the mine entrance.

Then Pancho remembered a story about the original Cid that someone had told him along the way. Indeed, he had learned much about the eleventh century hero whilst on his peregrinations with "the new Cid". And legend had it that after el Cid had been killed during his ultimate battle, to be victorious in Valencia, his men had the idea to construct a frame like the back of a chair on the rear of his horse Babieca's saddle, and then strap the dead Cid onto it, as though he were alive and riding the horse. Then, with an aide actually holding Bibieca's reins and thus guiding the horse and its apparently alive rider, el Cid was seen by all to lead his army out of their besieged castle and straight into the ranks of the enemy forces outside – men who had seen el Cid killed only a short time ago. Now, seeing a risen Cid leading his army once again, they panicked and fled the scene, thus giving the late Cid's side the victory.

So Pancho, using bungy cords from Bibieca's toolbox, strapped the still-unconscious Sidney into the driver's seat, and he got into the passenger seat. He then started the engine, put it in "drive" and, steering with his left hand and stretching his left foot over to operate the gas pedal and the brake, roared off toward the slowly advancing army of would-be gold thieves. The Jeep's top was down, so Sidney could clearly be seen behind the wheel. And he still wore his sunglasses, so no one could tell that his eyes were not open. Pancho drove Bibieca toward the eight leaders of the various groups, screaming invectives all the time.

When the aforementioned group leaders saw the vehicle of the so-called Cid, with a -- a living, resurrected Cid in the driver's seat(!), they all froze in their tracks, thinking this was the man they had all witnessed, from a distance of no more than one or two meters, shot directly in the heart and knocked to the ground, just a matter of minutes ago!

The ETX man crossed himself hurridly and cried out, "He lives! He is truly el Cid Campeador! We cannot fight an immortal! And we know what they say he did to Ali bin Belchin and the Sons of Allah! I and the men of ETX are not going to wait around and have him do the same to us!" Then he turned and shouted to his followers, "Run, men! El Cid is real! He has returned from the dead! He will kill us all if we dally! Run!"

The other group leaders looked at each other and then,

apparently deciding that discretion was the better part of valor, turned and yelled similar words to their own men. In the meantime, "el Cid" was seen to be driving Bibieca in circles through the rabble army, giving them all a chance to see the risen hero knight, returned from the eleventh century – and the dead. Screaming in fear, they all turned on their heels and ran. But even as they fled, one could hear the Anarchist and the Communist arguing violently with each other.

"You ran first!"

"No, you did!"

CHAPTER 37

Back in Madrid, a grateful king gave Sidney *un abrazo*, or Spanish "bear hug", as did the prime minister after him. Spain would now survive! The king read out the long list of deeds Sidney had made happen, in the order in which they had occurred:

- He had made the Spanish people aware of the monstrous plan to ring Spain with wind turbines, ruining the land's beautiful sea views and spoiling historical sites; that plan had now been "put on hold".

- He had urged the president of Cataluña to give up the preposterous plan of independence and had informed the world of such via the media.

- He had saved hundreds of lives in Barcelona, causing people to move away from the Telefónica just before a gas main exploded there.

- In "the Basque country" he had called upon all areas of Spain to shuck the ideas of devisiveness, in favor of a restored, great new Spain.

- He had thwarted the invasion of a new Napoleon from France, causing the capture of the fiend and recovering large sums of money stolen from the Bank of Spain.

- He had saved the great Cave of Altamira from destruction by men of the Partido de Chalados de Cantabria, who, acting on a false rumor, would blow up the irreplaceable treasure rather than have Americans move it to Disney World.

- He had escaped imprisonment and starvation at the hands of the pro-independence movement of Galicia, los Malucos.

- He had recovered the long lost, solid silver reliquary, *la Virgen y Niño con Pistola*, and presented it to the Archbishop of the Cathedral of Santiago de Compostela, where it was meant to be delivered from Mexico in 1877.

- He had saved the Alhambra in Granada from destruction by the Sons and Second Cousins of Allah, and had caused their demise.

- He had caused menacing men of the Soñadores Andalucistas to abandon nefarious plans in Granada.

- He had interrupted a visit by a delegation of bureaucrats of the European Union from Brussels, causing them to return home before they could cause any harm, inconvenience or embarrassment to Spain.

- He had located and recovered the Spanish government's entire gold bullion stockpile of 1936, thought to have disappeared in the Soviet Union.

- He had caused the dispersing of armed, massed groups who favored a broken-up and vastly weakened Spain, and whose intent it was to steal the gold of 1936.

- He had enabled Spain's debts to be paid off, resulting in unprecedented gains in the Spanish stock market.

But Sidney was not yet finished in his quest to make Spain great again. He now huddled with the two top men of the land and told them of his latest idea. The king and the PM came away wide-eyed and shaking their heads in wonder.

Yes, Sidney had indeed been immersed in Medieval Spanish Literature over the decades, yet he had not been *totally* unaware of things going on in the outside world. And although he could tick off a long list of wondrous accomplishments he had caused to happen on behalf of Spain, there was yet one thing that had not been achieved: Spain had still not regained her great empire, those fabulous colonies. But Sidney had an idea.

The new U.S. president was known to look askance at immigrants from poorer parts of the world – just look at the Mexican Wall, for example. Well, Puerto Ricans were also always flowing into the States, something made easier for them due to the fact that Puerto Rico was these days a "commonwealth" of the United States – whatever that was – and its citizens could enter the mainland far easier than could Mexicans or most anybody else from another country. So what if Puerto Rico were *not* a U.S. dependency?

Working on the basis of the president's concern – some said xenophobia – concerning immigration, Sidney proposed that Spain, with some of its newfound gold, *buy* Puerto Rico back from the U.S., and thus reestablish its empire, at least in part. After all, the United States had simply *taken* Puerto Rico from Spain at the end of the Spanish-American War of 1898. Not only would the U.S. government earn a lot of money which they could then throw away on some inane new idea(s), the move would cut off the flow of thousands – maybe millions – of Puerto Ricans coming into the U.S. proper.

Well, the U.S. president, after much thought and after many discussions with top advisors, following the transmission of the idea to him from the Secretary of State, decided to "go for the deal". A purchase price was reached with Spain (some Americans complained it was far too low), and, in a ceremony in Washington with the Spanish Minister of State and the Ambassador of Spain to the United States on the one hand, and the President and the Secretary of State on the other, a treaty was signed, hands shaken, and a check handed over. Subsequent riots in Puerto Rico were ignored for the time being, especially as the treaty provided for continued possession of U.S. military bases in perpetuity, as with Guantanamo Bay, in Cuba.

As the treaty-signing meeting broke up, the U.S. president could be heard to say in an aside to an aide. "Hell, I'd have *given* the damned place to 'em if they'd just asked for it!"

DRAWN
BY L. SLD CAMP —
AFTER MY ADVENTURE

Spain resumes control of Puerto Rico

CHAPTER 38

Time had passed, and now Sidney stood facing the king in the great Audience Hall of the palace in Madrid. Pancho stood some three paces back. The king pinned a medal – actually a welded conglomeration of fabulous, newly struck and beribboned medals – on Sidney's chest, in honor of his service to Spain. Even Pancho got a medal. The men from Brussels had been paid off and were now satisfied to leave Spain alone, and the nation's economy had been given a healthy shot in the arm. Not only that, but all those troublesome splinter groups seemed to have melted into the woodwork, as the saying goes. And, of course, Spain was an empire again. The people in Puerto Rico would surely come to accept things before too long, but their objections were of secondary importance. After all, had not their ancestors allowed the *yanquis* to steal the island in 1898?

Yes, the king was very happy. But the wiley fellow had a card up his sleeve, it seemed. With no one in the Audience Hall other than himself, the prime minister, Sidney and Pancho, he lowered his voice and spoke to Sidney. Things in Spain were going well, he said – for the present. And "while everything was quiet" he wanted to broach a new subject. In poring over the Spanish constitution, he said, he had found a little-known clause in it which permitted him, the king, to abdicate and to put in his place another personage of royal blood – *not necessarily of his family* – and to give that person emergency powers, if needs be, *even to dissolve the government in favor of direct rule.* At this last part, the prime minister gasped and goggled at the king, who then turned to Sidney and said, "And I would be honored if you would accept this new job, that of ruling Spain, under the title not of king, but as *el Cid Campeador II!*"

"But . . . but . . .he is not of royal blood!" blurted the PM, pointing at Sidney.

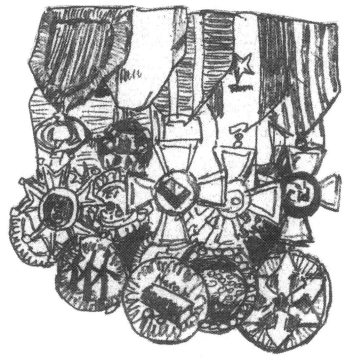

DRAWN
BY L. SID CAMP —
AFTER MY ADVENTURE

Medals from the King to Sidney

"And I will fix that!" replied the king, walking over to a Louis XV-looking chair on which lay a handsome, bejeweled sword. Picking up the long weapon, he pulled it from its scabbard and returned to face Sidney. *"Señor,"* he said gravely, "if you accept, I will dub you not only a knight of the realm, but I will also grant you the title of el Duque de Todo. You will have royal blood. Do you accept?

A stunned Sidney mumbled, *"Supongo qué si!* – I suppose so!" He dropped to his knees.

A smiling king then tapped Sidney on both shoulders and dubbed him the Duque de Todo. Sidney started to rise, but the king motioned him back down. Now, going to yet another chair off to the side, this one as Louis XV-looking as the other, from under a purple velvet cover he brought over the Royal Crown of Spain. "And I further proclaim you el Cid Campeador II, Absolute Ruler of all Spain! Tomorrow there will be an elaborate ceremony for the public and the media, but that will be just for show. As of this moment, you are, as you *yanquis* would say, 'the boss'. And now, if you will excuse me, my wife and I have some packing to do. We have always dreamed of living in a villa in Monaco. And Prince Albert is a friend of mine! He then shook hands all around, clapped his hands for an aide whom he briefly briefed, and turned to leave the great hall.

"But Your Majesty!" wailed the prime minister. "What about me?"

"Oh, of course, *Señor* Prime Minister! Thank you for all your work! Thank you *very* much!" He shook the PM's hand. And the ex-king departed, leaving a slack-jawed prime minister – and a newly arrived and dumbfounded aide -- to sort it all out. As he went out the door, Sidney heard the king say laughingly to one of his ex-flunkies, "And now I quit while I'm ahead!"

THE END

Printed in the United States
By Bookmasters